I0571912

BURNING WIND

A PRECIOUS REUBEN NOVEL

Burning Wind

Contact the author at: precyreuben@hotmail.com, or http://www.precious-fictions.com

Acknowledgment

Much appreciation goes to my friends and family, most especially my dear mum who has been very supportive in all I do. Special thanks go to my great friends who were ever-ready to listen to my ideas, and providing their time and encouragement when needed.

"Without support and encouragement, dreams are nothing more than thoughts hidden in the mind of the dreamer." – Precious Reuben.

Dedication

For

Charity C. Owoh

Still the most amazing woman I know.

Burning Wind

Chapter 1

North Quincy, Massachusetts, where Brenda lived, was a flourishing little town of Chinese-owned small businesses and corporate head offices. The workload at the small post office there was quickly dispatched by the swift services of Brenda and her colleagues. Properly dressed in grey polo, black pants, and red vests with their names and the company logo printed on the right side, the two other staff members alongside Brenda were cheerful as they responded speedily to customer needs.

The time was almost 5 p.m. and Brenda looked forward to closing for the day. She waited for a smiling old man dragging in a heavy box. "Please include a shipping confirmation as well," he said. He reached for his well-worn brown wallet and waited for her to announce the fee. She punched in the necessary information on the thick, touch-screen monitor and began peeling and pasting stickers on the box.

"Your total is fifty-five dollars and forty-nine cents, sir," she said wearily. She had been on her feet for hours as she processed shipping for more than fifty holiday-package bearing customers. She twisted from side to side trying to ease the aching pain in her feet. She collected the fee from the man and punched it into the register, which immediately popped out revealing stacks of dollar bills, neatly arranged. She brought out some dollar notes and coins.

"Here's your change," she replied, smiling wanly out of habit. "Do have a nice weekend," she concluded. The old man smiled, waved and walked away. She quickly left her post and went to the locker room where she began changing her clothes. The postal job was not what she had gotten a degree to do, but it paid the bills and kept her head above water. It would do for now until she could make other decisions.

She hadn't forgotten that her friends were coming over that evening. She was too tired to entertain anyone, but since it was their tradition to meet, gossip, and watch movies every Friday evening, she really couldn't object.

As she slipped into her faded jeans and green wool sweater with a silky yellow scarf wrapped round her neck, she grabbed her tote bag and walked into the main office, heading for the time clock. She brought out a card with her name on it, gently inserting it and waiting for a confirmation of her closing time. She put the card back in the holding box on the side, waved at her colleagues, and walked away.

Brenda walked a couple of blocks from postal center on the dirty, snow-covered busy road, stopping by a grocery store managed by a middle aged Chinese man. She picked up some drinks and her favorite ice cream along with some international prepaid calling cards. She paid for them without exchanging pleasantries with the proprietor. She simply was too tired.

Arriving home, she noticed a medium sized box wrapped in brown paper in front of her door. She didn't quite know what to make of it as she wasn't expecting an early Christmas gift. Curiously, she walked closer to the box, turned it to the labeled side and read her name on the slip.

Still bemused, she brought the box into her small, scantily furnished living room apartment. It was what the budget of an hourly paid employee would bear. A second-hand couch, a glass coffee table she had bought from one of her colleagues who was relocating, and on a small mahogany shelf, a 32" inch flat screen TV--the sum of her furnishings. She wasn't the type to decorate as long as she was comfortable, and she didn't expect to be there forever anyway. She walked quickly to the small kitchen where pots and pans hung above the stove area. That was her friend Toni's idea of an adorable kitchen fit for a woman her age. Toni had visited her one weekend and insisted on tidying the kitchen to her tasteful standard. She ordered the white oak kitchen table to be replaced with a modern-looking brick top. This upgrade made the kitchen the most interesting room in her apartment.

As Brenda glanced around the kitchen, she recognized the smell of unwashed dishes and pans stacked in the sink. She pulled out one of the bottom drawers and dashed out with a knife. She ran the sharp edge of the knife along the sealed tape on the mystery box, and digging through the packing material, brought out a heavy, colorful box with a picture of a laptop computer on it.

"I didn't order any PC," she muttered. Still unsatisfied, she scuffled through her tote bag and brought out her cell phone. She began dialing the number on the shipping label and listened.

"Thank you for calling Worldwide Shippers, my name is Jake, ID number 4459. How may I help you today?" the voice echoed in her ears.

"I just received a package which I didn't order. I do not see the sender information either, yet it's addressed to me. May I know who sent it?" she asked impatiently to the waiting voice on the other line.

"Absolutely ma'am," May I have the reference number on the box?"

"G23955pu601," she pronounced loudly.

"Thank you," came the polite response.

Even though she always admired the courteous response of those customer service people on the phone, she wasn't in the mood to hear it all today.

"I see that this package is for Ms. Brenda Akin. Address, 230 Norway Drive, Quincy..."

"Yes! That's the problem," she interrupted. "That's my name and address, but can you tell me who sent it?"

The agent drew a long breath, absorbing her previous interruption and continued, "I see here that the package was shipped from the manufacturer so I'm guessing the sender didn't include the purchaser's name. Do you want the number of the manufacturer so they can help you further with this issue?"

While the voice inquired, Brenda thought about Edward and his ever creative ways of enticing her.

"Lord! Why didn't I think of him? Who else would do such a thing?" she whispered to herself.

"Oh no, that will be all. Thank you," she replied to the voice.

"Well thank you for calling and have a good day."

She disconnected the call. Still anxious about the package, she began pulling the inner box free of the Styrofoam packing around it and revealed a black Dell laptop. She opened it and was exultant as the screen came alive, welcoming her.

She was completely absorbed in setting up the new laptop and didn't hear the knock on the door. The third knock shook her as she quickly gathered the littered plastic wrappers on the floor. She picked up the laptop and ran to her room to hide it away, eager to revisit it later.

"Hey girl," Toni hailed, flinging her red purse in the air and squeezing her way past Brenda. "You got someone in here, "cause my knuckles are sore from knocking," Toni exclaimed as she pulled at the hem of her tight orange wool sweater which stretched further each time she raised her arm. Her tight leather pants made her look like she was attending a Bonnie Am concert, and her puffed up

Afro moved with every turn. She quickly adjusted the weave as she turned to sit on the sofa, rubbing off some of her sky blue eye shadow and heavy face powder in the process. She was in her late twenties with extra pounds on her from coming to America and living in luxury. Careful not to split her pants, she gently lowered herself which pushed her mid-section above her waistline in an unpleasant manner.

"Let me guess, you forgot we were coming?" Alex, who had come in right behind Toni, inquired as he slumped into the couch himself, tossing his tight leather blazer open to reveal a pink knight sweater and black pants which looked as though they had been pressed with an overheated iron. His haircut complimented his light-skinned face. Alex's nose stood out from his face like that of early English men. He sat and crossed his right leg over the left smoothly and spread his arms on the couch majestically.

"Sweetie how was work today? God, you look exhausted!" he declared, getting up to feel Brenda's forehead with the back of his hand as if to detect some illness.

"If I tell you that you are allowing yourself to suffer like this because you do not want to have anything to do with your husband, you'll probably throw me out."

Brenda had barely said a word. She kept thinking of the gift in her bedroom. She didn't know if it was the right time to share it with her friends and succumb to Toni's harsh criticism or simply to listen to Alex blame her for every headache that she got. Either way, she knew she had to keep it to herself until she found out who the real sender was. She moved toward the kitchen.

"How did your interview go this morning, Alex?" Brenda inquired as she emerged with three spoons and a carton of *Haagen Dazs* ice cream.

"Hun, you won't believe what happened to me today," Alex began.

Brenda and Toni listened with interest as they scooped the ice cream from the carton. "I went to the office all dressed up---trust me, God! You won't believe who was gonna interview me."

Toni shifted her attention like she knew where the conversation was headed. They both knew that Alex's stories always ended with meeting a new man each week, even his father. The thing that fascinated Brenda about Alex was his boisterous and outgoing nature. His feminine side always added a twist to his humor.

The friends always met to escape their solitude.

"Oh….he had those looks of Idris Elba. You know Idris Elba right?" Alex described.

"Mmhmm," Brenda nodded with interest. She always enjoyed Alex's precise descriptions. At least he was lucky to meet all sorts of men he liked.

"Then he asked me for a drink tomorrow," Alex continued. "And I'm guessing you refused the offer, right?" Toni teased. "What? Refuse a drink? Well I wouldn't do that because I am still single and looking," he retorted to Brenda who sighed and glared at him from the corner of her eye.

The evening gathering wasn't like their usual chattering evening because Brenda just wasn't of the right disposition that night. The rest of the evening was spent watching a movie, a soap opera and finally, arguing over a fashion show on TV. They left before midnight and Brenda retired to bed.

At the crack of dawn, Brenda was awake in her bed and planning her day. It was a sluggish Saturday morning as she heard the cruel sound of lovemaking coming from her neighbors' apartment. It reminded her of her loneliness. This time the pounding was ferocious unlike the other days when they were done before she knew what was going on. The shrill whimper from the woman thrilled Brenda. It was as if the woman was being pinned down to the floor with the man's palm wrapped around her neck. She tried to imagine herself and Edward in such an orgasmic scenario but quivered in rejection of the thought. She didn't know why she suddenly hated everything about him.

She hurriedly got up, nearly forgetting about the laptop. But she bent down in front of her bed and dragged it gently out of its box to take a better look at the device. She looked inside and found an envelope neatly attached to the box.

"How come I didn't notice that before making all those goddamned calls?," she cursed.

"Hope you like it?," the note read. "Permit me to see your beautiful face again. Love, Edward." Her heart raced and her perplexity set in. She read the note over again as if it contained some sort of secret code. She fumed angrily and decided it was time to set things straight.

She reached for her cell phone and began punching in the numbers vigorously. She waited impatiently for a voice to come on the line, but she heard an automated message instructing her to leave a voice message. She slammed the phone down, and exhaled anger from her nostrils, batting her eyes lids irritatingly. She decided to try a second time, thinking fervently that the pranks Edward was playing on her needed to be stopped that moment. To her dissatisfaction, the call went straight to voice mail again. She tossed the phone across the bed and walked into the bathroom mumbling to herself.

Chapter 2

The yellow telephone in the kitchen chimed endlessly. Brenda dashed out of the bathroom with a towel wrapped around her rotund waist, revealing her long legs. Her round face was covered with her facial mask, exposing only her eyes. She quickly yanked the phone off the hook and inhaled as she said, "Hello?"

The other voice responded with, "Good morning, Angel. Hope you slept well last night. I called your cell phone a couple of times with no response. When are you coming home, Sweetie?" the baritone voice sang.

"Hello?" She repeated herself as if she didn't hear what the caller had said.

"Brenda, it's me Edward. I hope the gift I sent was to your taste?" the voice continued.

"What do you think you are doing by sending me a gift?" she screamed into the phone. "Who put you up to this? I told you that I shall return when I'm ready, so sending me a gift is a complete waste of time. Why can't you just leave me alone?" she shrieked.

"I've been longing to see your beautiful face again. I'm not trying to force you to come back. Just felt that the kids and I should have a means of seeing you. At least they do not deserve this treatment," Edward rejoined calmly, ignoring his wife's rants. "The kids want to visit you. Would you mind if I accompany them?"

"Accompany them? Why? The last thing I want to do is to set my eyes on you right now."

"Why are you being so bullheaded? They are your children, and even if you do not want to forgive their father, then you can at least show them some love."

"Are you trying to say that I don't love my children?"

"No, no. That's not what I meant," Edward responded quickly, beginning to betray the frustration in his voice. "Let's resolve this as quickly as we can. Do you want a divorce then?"

"Do your worst. I don't care about anything you wish to do, Edward." Brenda snapped the phone and stomped into her bedroom, her face crumpled in anger and sorrow.

As Brenda sat by the cold window of the airplane, she thought about how unhappy she'd been in the past few years and how much she had anticipated this trip to the United States at last. She had written the love story of her life in the most complicated manner.

She was diverted from her thoughts by the cries of a baby whose mother was struggling to hush the child as she smiled apologetically at the other passengers stirred by the loud cry. Brenda watched from the corner of her eye as the woman succeeded in restoring the tranquil atmosphere. The woman began humming and tapping her feet gently as she rocked the baby who seemed to be enjoying the attention.

It reminded her so much of when her twins were babies--the twins she had just abandoned. She hadn't planned for things to turn out this way, but since this was the only means she had to reclaim her freedom as a woman, then not even her children would stand in her way. She was drawn back to her thoughts of how unhappy yet relieved she was.

It was already two o'clock on a cold rainy Saturday afternoon as Brenda and her parents ambled toward the four year old green Toyota 4Runner. She was dressed in a red, black, and white plaid skirt with a white short-sleeved shirt and a small cravat around her neck. These flattered her neatly braided hair which was gathered in a pony tail. It was a typical school uniform for private high schools in Nigeria then. Chief Akin, swathed in a vast lacy green agbada with a round cap sitting on his head, commanded Ojo, the middle-aged gate man, to load Brenda's luggage in the trunk of the car. Mrs. Akin was talking on her cell phone as she beamed at her frowning young daughter. "Sweetie, I hope you have everything you'll need for the semester?" Mrs. Akin inquired. The daughter nodded in response but was still unhappy. Everyone buckled themselves into the car which gently glided away from the large, white three-story mansion complemented by the gold-framed windows. Light red and grey marble graced every corner of the estate with a fleet of cars parked in the left corner. The fleet was shielded from the sun by a dark blue shade surrounded by a modern meshed gate.

The servants all lined up outside, waving cheerfully at the car as it drove off the compound. People often compared their house to the White House in Washington D.C. because it stood as the most elegant and exquisite architecture in the city. Many times, people would drive by her house just to be inspired for their own homes. There had been gossip that Brenda's father had contacted a German architect on one of his trips to Holland to assist him in creating the perfect building plan.

At fourteen, Brenda Akin had been admitted into the prestigious Queen's Girls High School, a boarding school about thirty miles from her home. She had just graduated from primary school and was not overly excited about the new school. There had been stories that only the affluent could afford to send their children to such a place. The tuition fee was what some families lived on in a year.

Brenda wasn't excited by the idea of leaving her parents to come to this unknown place, all in the name of study. It was a challenging phase for her. She spent most of her weekends at home with their housemaid since her parents were always traveling for business. She enjoyed having her friends over for movies, but now her fun would be cut short because she would only visit home once or twice a semester. Moreover, most of her friends had been sent to study abroad by their affluent parents, so the thought of having to make new friends worried her the most.

They drove for forty minutes and pulled into a magnificent compound with marvelous edifices surrounded by rich green turf. The administrative quarters were painted sky blue with silver crowns. Each structure was as well detailed as if the Queen herself lived there. The main gate held pennants from different countries that fluttered moderately with the wind.

The compound was crammed with all brands of automobiles as if it were an auto-dealers' store front. The school gateman, well dressed in his dark blue beret and green suit, saluted reverentially at the cars that trooped into the compound. Girls her age, with all manner of looks, sauntered behind their parents into the large welcome hall. Matrons beamed as they stood waiting, their arms folded behind them.

The newcomers assembled before a large table with wooden clipboards and check sheets in the corner. The table was covered with a large banner indicating the school's motto. "Excellence in knowledge." Each student's luggage was checked to confirm that the contents met the obligatory requirements, and the parents were respectfully informed of anything that was missing and how important it was that they send it immediately. Once the checklist was complete, a tour guide led the families through the corridor to the dormitories.

Brenda received no exception at this check point. She waited patiently as the matron rummaged through her luggage. She then walked through a vast hall with large framed photos of virtuosos and exceptional alumni on both sides of the sky-blue hallway. One's picture was hung there only if one brought an honor to the school. Brenda imagined her face on one of the frames with a big smile. Perhaps she'd be the winner someday in the national spelling competition which was held annually. She was carried away by her reverie when she came in contact with Lady C. Briggs, the school principal.

Lady C. Briggs was a brilliant, petite middle aged lady who oversaw the affairs of the girls in the school. She was a disciplined woman with a heavy-handed persona. Without mincing words, she wouldn't hesitate to expel anyone who contravened the rules. Her colleagues referred to her as the Margaret Thatcher of Queen's College.

She was standing at the far right corner of a furnished room with a twin bed in each corner, holding a small folder in one hand and a pen at the other. She was clad in a white long sleeved shirt with a knee-length black pencil skirt, her dark colored weave neatly brushed by the side and a lorgnette which sat loosely on her pointed nose.

"Hello Sir, madam," she nodded toward the parents. "Welcome once again, Miss Akin. My name is Lady C. Briggs, but you can call me Lady Briggs. Fortunately, you are the first to arrive in this room, so you may choose a bed. Here's a booklet of the academic policy and direction which we shall discuss later with others once you settle in," she said, offering the document to Brenda.

"Dinner is at seven in the cafeteria. No food is to be brought back from the cafeteria, but you may have snacks which you have purchased or are sent to you from home."

"My office is located in the admin quarters of the school," she continued, hardly pausing to breathe. "Any questions?" she asked, crisply. Brenda and her parents glanced at each other, but no one responded.

"Your room mates should be arriving any time now. Make sure you read this book before Monday for appropriate guidance. Have a pleasant day," upon which Lady C. Briggs turned on her heel and exited the room.

Brenda's mother winked at her daughter as if she would explode in laughter as the lady walked away. "Now you are in school..." she exclaimed.

Brenda was astonished at such a presentation from the lady she had heard so much about. She went to hug her father who had been standing there quietly with a smile on his face. "Thank you, Daddy," she said as she wrapped her arms around him.

Her mother walked up to her and kissed her forehead. "Be good my dear. Make sure you charge your phone always as we'll be calling you daily. Be a good girl, okay? I love you."

Brenda watched them from her room window as they drove out of the compound. She slumped into the bed in the corner she had chosen, and her eyes caught the quotes from former students, written on the ceiling. She was surprised they hadn't been painted over.

She left her luggage strewn in the middle of the room. She had dozed off for a couple of minutes when three other girls came in to the room, unaccompanied by parents.

One of the girls, Rita, spied Brenda napping. "Excuse me....Hello...are you there?" Rita yelled at Brenda. "How many corners do you plan to occupy during your stay here? Do you mind moving your things to one corner so I can unpack, miss...?" Rita shouted again, chewing her gum sarcastically.

Rita was a tall, dark-skinned girl who had a body with all the curves in the right places and a tongue as sharp as a battle sword. She was dressed in a tight blue jeans, yellow logoed shirt and black poplin shoes with white laces. She continuously popped her bubble gum loudly.

Staring boorishly at Brenda, she turned to the two other girls in the room and asked, "What's wrong with her?"

The other two girls ignored her. They watched from the corner of their eyes as she turned to Brenda who began moving her boxes out of the way. The girls looked like they were afraid of her; she then sat on her bed and began unpacking quietly.

That was not the type of introduction she had expected from her roommates. It dawned on her that she was about to share a room with strangers, and apparently, arrogant strangers. Soon the other rooms were filled with students clamoring and running up and down the stairs. The school bell was heard from afar, at the center of the school. All the students began trooping out of their rooms and headed towards the meeting hall to which the bell was summoning them.

Chapter 3

The vast school hall was designed with huge poles on two sides of the room with a short stair leading to the podium, and a large badge situated behind an orange lighted glass. The rays of the evening sun pointed to the floor before the students, painting a faint shadow of the podium. The faculty and staff all lined up on the left corner before the students. The black and white painted statues of intellectuals and late Nigerian leaders, balanced the academic look of the hall.

All the students lined up leaving a wide gap in the center of the room. They clamored in a mellow tone which was short-lived as Lady C. Briggs walked into the hall and marched to the podium. The room was so quiet that a pin drop could be heard from afar. She stood before them with a stern look on her face as if a student had violated the eleventh commandment in the Bible. She stared at the quiet hall for a second and then began her speech.

"Tradition, honor and discipline; these are the three pillars of Queen's Girls High school," she began. "The values with which will shape your future. Those who have preceded you have set very high standards for you. Today, all of them are successful women in their respective fields. Some are great doctors, engineers, lawyers, respected businesswomen, and some, great politicians. But all of them have one thing in common; all their lives they have followed the principles taught to them by this great school. Today, you have the opportunity to be a part of this great lineage. You've been selected from all over the country and brought here, because we believe that you have what it takes to be great women.

"Success does not come easy," she continued. "Behind every success lies great sacrifice. By entering this institution today, you have shut yourself from the outside world. We expect that you will work with full concentration and with strict discipline. If anyone is found guilty of misconduct, she will be expelled immediately. And remember one thing, once you are expelled from here, the doors of all other educational institutions would be shut from you forever. So if there is anyone here unwilling to make this sacrifice, she is free to walk out that gate right now. But if you have decided to stay, then that gate and the world outside does not exist for you anymore. Now I want all of you to close your eyes and bow your heads and think about every word I've said and make your own decision." Silence reigned as the students immediately bowed their heads as commanded. The speech was concluded with, "Welcome once again to Queen's Girls School" With that, the Lady Briggs marched out of the hall with the faculty trooping behind her, whereupon the noise resumed.

As they departed from the hall, Rita walked up to her with a smile. "Hey, I'm sorry about my attitude towards you earlier. I guess we started off on the wrong foot. "My name is Rita Azinga," she began.

"I'm Brenda Akin," Brenda responded.

"I guess we could be friends as long as you don't block my entry again?" Rita pleaded with a smile. The two girls laughed and chatted further as they returned to their room to finish unpacking.

On Monday morning the girls hastily dressed in their school uniforms and proceeded towards the large school refectory. They found the hall neatly arranged with tall, spacious mahogany tables lined up side by side with pink plastic table cloths. The kitchen staff, neatly dressed in white gowns and caps, wordlessly placed each food tray. In less than five minutes, the hall was swarming with over one hundred girls ready for breakfast. Late arrivals scampered into the hall, scavenging for the last few seats. As the girls sat down, a clatter arose. Clatter and scurry seemed to be the primary conceit of the dining hall.

Brenda sat throughout her first lecture, thinking of her parents. She missed home and found the boarding life humdrum. Making friends wasn't that easy as it seemed like everyone already had their friends from their former schools. Some girls were naturally gregarious and didn't seem to need friends.

Suddenly, her thoughts were interrupted when a sudden silence fell over the classroom.
The door opened, and the seniors marched into the class room to eye the freshmen. It was a mark of respect for the juniors to respect the seniors, especially those in leadership roles.

Brenda had heard rumors about how seniors often lured younger students to become their 'school-daughters'. The way she heard it, it was customary for most private and government schools then. Of course there were horrific stories of how these seniors turned their so-called students into lesbian lovers in return for cash and protection from the more bullying senior girls. But most who passed through this "school-daughter" rite mostly told how their 'school-mothers' took good care of them at school, provided for them, and in return, they would run little errands for them. Most of them confessed that the main reason why they agreed to become school-daughters is because they needed protection from the more intimidating seniors.

If during the selection process, a younger student refused, she would face despicable treatment from the other seniors. Like a chick, she would be left to defend for herself from the birds of prey.

Of course the school authorities did not support this treatment and encouraged students to come forward and report any form of ill treatment or felt-oppression they may have experienced from their seniors. This only made matters worse because the seniors didn't hesitate to retaliate in the most menacing of manners.

The terrified students, declining to mention the ordeals to their parents either, instead embraced the behavior as a rite of passage which made boarding life more interesting than anything else. Sometimes, the freshmen even made the first move to the seniors they admired the most, seeking their acceptance as their school daughters. Despite rumors and fears, it could be a fantastic experience for some who were lucky to be under the wings of truly role-model-worthy seniors.

Brenda watched the more mature girls in their short plaid skirts and white, short-sleeved shirts, parade around the class as if they owned the school. They glanced on their lists and selected the beautiful ones from wealthy families because they would gain more from this than they would have to spend on them instead. Brenda felt lucky that she was not selected, for some reason best known to the seniors, nor was she disappointed because she had no expectations. Perhaps, she thought, no one knew about her parents' status in the community, or maybe it was simply her inconspicuousness.

As she returned to her dormitory, she noticed Rita calling out her name and walking swiftly towards her. "You know if I hadn't met you before, I'd say you were deaf," she said, rolling her eyes. "Come to think of it, do we have any handicapped students here? I mean does this school make provisions for that?" Rita asked with an asinine look on her face.

Brenda laughed out loud as she listened to her friend natter. "Not to be sarcastic, but think of it this way, if we had deaf and blind people around, how do you think they would cope with the likes of Lady Briggs appearing every second like a ghost? I think they would all regain their senses with the way that lady speaks." she continued.

"You've met her already?" Brenda inquired.

"Who hasn't?" Rita continued. "The lady is like the *god* of this school. My eldest sister who graduated here years ago told me horrible things about her. One could even write a book about that lady." Brenda listened with curiosity.

"I heard she was in the German Army School," Rita gossiped, "where her father worked as the drill officer. If you look at the way she walks, it's like she's marching to war. The woman never laughs."

Brenda burst out laughing with tears in her eyes. Just when she thought that this school wasn't exciting at all, she found the perfect girl to entertain her.

"Oh my God!" Brenda laughed, conspiratorially. "I don't think she's that bad like you make her seem. I just see a much disciplined woman who aspires for the best in her students. One can't blame her you know. Did your sister also mentioned if she was married or not?" Brenda queried. She was very much interested in getting to know more about Lady Briggs, mostly to keep out of her way.

"Three times!" Rita demonstrated with her fingers. "I heard she was once married to an Italian business man but she divorced him when she found out he had a mistress."

"So that's justifiable then?"

"Well, you can say that but I wouldn't be so wobbly before her.

"Does she even have children?"

"*For where*? I heard that was one of the reasons why her husband left her. She doesn't want children because it would interrupt her career,"

"Wow. You seem to know a lot about this lady?"

"Don't you read the City People magazine? Haven't you read her stories in one of them? Anyways, let's drop her issue for now. Have you been to the boy's campus before?" Rita asked with a covetous look on her face.

"No, where is it?"

"Come with me and let me show you something interesting," Rita beckoned.

They walked towards the back yard of the admin quarters. She climbed on an old slab which enabled her see the other side of the wall. "There...," she pointed to a large compound built like theirs too. There was a remarkable resemblance between the campuses.

"That's where the boys live," Rita winked at stunned Brenda who continued to stare, unblinking.

"Wow! I didn't know they had 'brother' school too, but why so close to ours?'

"Duh, because men and women need to stay together!" Rita retorted with a sarcastic laugh.

"Do they ever visit?" "Yeah...sometimes... or on an errand with a supervisor."

"What does that mean?"

"It means that they don't come here unless they were invited on an academic mission.

"Don't you see the fine print? Boys and young girls equals girls gone wild!" Brenda spelt out. Here she was thinking that this school was filled with lots of dreary students, including herself, not realizing that there were also lax students as well. She knew enough to know that the combined school was a wrong move. How Rita knew everything in the school was an enigma to Brenda.

"So do you have any boyfriend from another school?" Rita wanted to know.

"No. I'm too young for that, and so are you," Brenda preached.

"Whatever, Mahatma Gandhi," Rita retorted as Brenda stared at her. "I have a boyfriend in that school. We went to primary school together and got admitted here as well. How fun, right?" she concluded smacking her lips.

"But you'll never have the opportunity to see him," Brenda concluded.

"Says who?" Rita retorted. "We see each other from time to time, and we exchange letters as well."

Brenda listened as she rambled. She had learnt more than enough in one day from this girl, but she couldn't help liking her witty character.

"Guess what?" Rita prattled on. "I heard the seniors are planning a social night event next week. I also heard that the senior boys are going to be there."

"Rita!" Brenda exclaimed, uncertain that her horror wasn't genuine.

"What? Don't you like parties? I haven't attended any since I came to this rehabilitation camp. Chill, girlfriend," she said as she saw the consternation on Brenda's face. "You only have one life to live, so you better start making use of it."

"But you heard Lady Briggs at the assembly right? I do not want to stand before that lady for any reason whatsoever."

"So what? She made a speech," Rita shrugged. "I mean we are not going to run away are we? So are you coming to the party or not?"

"Are freshmen invited as well?"

"Not really, but if you have a senior school mother then you've gained yourself a VIP invitation. Don't you have one yet?"

"No I don't," Brenda replied, a little defensively.

"Then you need to come. I also heard seniors make selections there too. Don't worry, it's a tradition and Lady Briggs can't change that."

Chapter 4

Every last Saturday of the month is the parents' visiting day. In the evening, the senior girls always hosted a party. The senior boys were allowed to the party for only a short period, under the watchful eye of their boarding master. It was eight o'clock as Rita got ready for the party, donning a short denim skirt with a pink tank top. She slipped into a pair of sandals with her hair pulled up into a pony tail. She waited impatiently for Brenda who dressed listlessly in a purple dress and sandals.

Brenda glanced around the dormitory in fear as they sidled along the hallways. Her heart raced, but the adventure on which she embarked with her daring friend was exciting. The two girls sneaked through the backdoor that led to the senior student lounge. The sound-proofed door shielded the loud music playing in the lounge.

The senior girls were all dressed in diminutive attire designed to accentuate their youthful curves. They wore light application of lip gloss and pancake makeup, which was only allowed for that night. Some daring ones ventured to eyeliner and mascara, drawing attention to their lovely eyes. The boarding mistress stood at the far corner of the hall watching the students mingle. The boys soon strode into the large room clad in shirts, long pants and leather shoes. They greeted and began to chat with the females they knew. Their boarding master stood alongside the boarding mistress, watching every move. The students timidly ate the chips which labored the tables, drank sodas, and danced until their feet ached.

Brenda was having a wonderful time, even though she sat at a corner the whole time, afraid of being asked to dance. She laughed when one of the boys danced stupidly in front a girl who quietly left him on the dance floor.

The party was interrupted when one of the senior boys called Nedu had found a love letter written by his roommate to a girl he admired. When he confronted the boy about the letter, the boy ignored him. This infuriated Nedu so much that he punched the boy in the face. This sent the boy tumbling to the floor in the presence of his fellow seniors, who engaged him to retaliate.

The boy sprang up, and although he was noticeably the weaker of the two, he sent a sharp blow to Nedu's chin. The short fight, which drew lots of attention, was quickly ended by a blow from the boarding master's long cane lashing the two men in the back. The boys rubbed at the stinging pain from the cane and frowned at each other. They knew it would bruise later.

The party was called off and the girls returned to their dormitories. Brenda hadn't seen the faces of the sparring young men due to the crowd that gathered around them that night. She wondered what the fate of the two boys would be on Monday morning when they would arraigned before their own principal, and most importantly, what the future of the social night would be for them all since the first one didn't end so well.

Weeks rolled into months and the semester came to an end. Cars were lined up just like that very first day as parents came to pick up their daughters after a long semester. Some parents sent drivers for the errand.

It was getting dark as Brenda sat in the lobby of her dormitory with her duffle bag, waiting for her parents. They had called to say they would be there around five, but it was already 6:30 with no sight of them. Worried that they might have forgotten to come, she strolled into the school park for some fresh air. Darkness was already creeping into the day as the last rays of sunlight streamed into the lonely park.

Nedu knew he wasn't going home that day. His mother had called to inform him that she would pick him up the next day instead. This has always been the case with him each holiday. He either went home earlier, later, or not at all. Sometimes he would stay with his other friends who weren't going home for the holidays. Sometimes they kept him company, not telling their parents about the holiday. So occasions like this permitted them to soar beyond the boundaries.

On this particular Friday evening, however, Nedu had no friends to keep him company as all his friends had gone home, so embracing his providence, he decided to climb over the fence that led to the girls' school. He wasn't expecting to see anyone at the girls' compound since it was a home weekend.

His friends had always dared him to go into the girls' school without the principal's permission. This was one of those games they played when they were alone. He knew this was the only opportunity he had to exert his courage without getting caught. He meandered towards the admin block, careful not to attract the gateman's attention. He turned to his left towards the tree-shaded park where the foliage was just thick enough to prevent sunlight from invading the cozy area. Students sometimes go there to study, chat, or just play with their friends during leisure time. He knew the penalty for his exploit if caught, yet he continued.

Standing behind the tall mango tree, he noticed Brenda sitting with a worried look on her face as she continuously pushed the buttons on her cell phone, and then placed it to her ear.

Brenda must have felt the presence of someone behind her as she turned anxiously. She peeped to see who it was, but it was too dark for her to see anything. The figure moved closer which made her take a few steps backwards with trepidation.

"Hello," a voice spoke full of anticipation. Still frightened, she peered into the darkness to catch a glimpse of his face. He probably wasn't there to hurt her, she thought. After all it was a school compound and only female students or administration staffs are allowed in the park at that time of the day. She remembered one of Rita's stories about how the boys would climb over the fence to meet their girlfriends secretly. "Maybe he's waiting for someone," she suggested to herself in an effort to calm her anxiety.

Nedu knew that there were lots of beautiful girls in the school but he wasn't always lucky to have one because of his shyness and sarcasm when it came to getting a girl. The last one he had his eye on set a bandage on his chin when a fight had ensued at the last party. His tall, slim body always attracted the yearning eyes of the girls each time he visited the school on special duties for the principal, but somehow, his approach always ruined it for him. But like any handsome teenager, he enjoyed the compliment from catching the eyes of the girls. He was only sixteen but already had the well-sculpted body of a Calvin Klein model.

He had been careful not to get caught wandering around the compound, but if there was anything that was worth the risk, it was the presence of this young girl whom he had never had the pleasure of meeting, standing here in the dark. The light from the setting moon was behind the tree, thereby inscribing her figure in shadows.

He felt oddly and abruptly attracted to this girl, aroused even, although he could barely see her face. Sensing fear in her breath, he drew closer to her. Unexpectedly, he grabbed her hand, pulling her closer and kissing her as she tried to escape him. She swept a harsh slap across his face and tried to run, but the muscular arms pulled her back to his front. As if a beast in him was awakened, he pushed her to the ground and began ripping off her shirt. He yanked off her bra and quickly covered her mouth with his left palm. He then unfastened his belt with the other hand. Still pinning her to the ground, he swept a harsh slap across her face to silence her whimpering. He vehemently spread her legs, still kneeling and pushed his hips in between them. Brenda shrieked out loud when she felt the painful tear in her vagina. He rode her ferociously, not minding her cries. He groaned inaudibly as he pummeled her. He came quickly, and, as if coming to from some kind of stupor, he realized with horror what he had done and quickly sprang to his feet. He stared at her as though he had just found a victim of someone else's rape. He quickly ran off struggling to buckle his belt, leaving Brenda, who had stopped fighting him, lying comatose on the ground.

Chapter 5

Chief Akin fumed in anger when he received the call from the school concerning his daughter's assault. He rushed to the hospital with his wife, stepping with all his weight as a Chieftain into the corridor where his daughter lay. He demanded to be led to her at once. The nurse, in turn, demanded his name in order to direct him to the right ward. His wife was halfway to the ward while her husband and the nurse jockeyed for authority. Realizing that seeing his daughter was the important issue, he answered quickly and was led into the narrow hospital corridor. The hall had the taint of illness. He bumped into two nurses as he hurried to his daughter's ward. Her mother sobbed uncontrollably as she saw her daughter in her unconscious state. She fell into her husband arms.

After observing his comatose daughter, Chief Akin dashed out of the hospital and headed to the police station.

Brenda had been unconscious for two days and finally woke up to see her mother's troubled face, standing over her.

"Doctor, she's awake!" Mrs. Akin shouted in exhilaration.

She yelled across the hallway for the nurses who came running into the room. The nurse observed Brenda quickly. "I'll get the doctor," she said, and walked away briskly. Brenda had awoken with a harsh headache, and she winced at every spoken word.

A few hours later, Chief Akin stomped into the ward with two policemen. They had come to take her statement to enable their search. Unfortunately, there was little that Brenda could tell the curious police officers who queried her because she neither recognized the face of her rapist nor knew where he had come from. The officers walked away dissatisfied with the information they received.

Chief Akin's irrepressible anger shook the entire school. He threatened everyone from the kitchen staff to the principal. He sent policemen who searched relentlessly for his daughter's rapist. Police dogs were unleashed as well to sniff out the culprit wherever he was. The news of the incident spread round the school like wildfire.

Lady C. Briggs was in her office reading from a flat screen monitor on her desk. There were portraits of her and her family huddled together in one corner of the wall. Her certificates and licenses were assembled on the other side beside a huge free-standing book shelf near her work desk. She was deeply engrossed in the online news she loved to read every morning while she sipped her coffee, when a man introducing himself as Det. Nicolas walked into her office. Her eyes dimmed and her face darkened in anger at the interruption.

"What is the meaning of this?" she barked. "How dare you stomp into my office at this hour," she said, narrowing her eyes.

The private detective responded quietly, ignoring Lady Briggs' anger. "A rape had been committed on your school ground and we require your cooperation, Ms. Briggs."

"Lady C. Briggs to you, Detective. A prior appointment might have been appropriate, don't you think? I've already informed you I will not speak to anyone aside from the police. As you can see, they are already on the case and I've told them everything they need to know to apprehend the perpetrator. Go back and tell your boss that we only have to follow necessary protocol to resolve this matter. I will not hesitate to inform you as soon as I hear the report from the police. I'd advise you stay away from my school and students for now. Extend my apologies once again to Chief Akin."

"We have learned that the rapist may have come from the boy's school. I only request that you give me the records of all the students, so that I can forward them to the police," the detective continued.

A guessing game was the only game the local police knew how to play when it came to solving a complicated crime as this. A mass arrest would be issued. If all the boys from the school were arrest and tortured, who knows, someone who wanted to escape the pain would sing to the policemen, and *voila!* A crime has been solved, the criminal would be arrested, and the city at peace.

Normally, with the amount of money Chief Akin promised Det. Nicholas, if he found the rapist, it was only a matter of time before he would present the rapist, dead or alive. But this was a different case, a very tough one.

Nicholas had been very excited the moment he received a call from Chief Akin to help investigate the matter in case the police had missed something. Chief Akin had felt that with an extra set of hands alongside the dawdling investigation of the police, Det. Nicolas might be able get to the bottom of it independently. The Chief couldn't wait to deal with the boy. Det. Nicolas had done minor investigations for Akin in the past and hadn't made as much money as he expected, so this time around he would be sure to devote his entire mind to the case which could earn him more. Luckily he was ahead of the police by already finding out where the rapist may have come from, but he seemed to be discouraged by the blasé response he was getting from the principal.

"I am not in charge of the boy's school," Lady Briggs rejoined. "However, those records are confidential information, and this school would be violating the rights of the students by doing that. Let the police investigator in charge come for these documents. We have over two-thousand students in this school and without proper evidence; I doubt you will be successful. I cannot hand you the files of all the boys in that school. What do you intend to do with them? Arrest them all or ask them if they've raped a girl? Let me remind you that this is a prestigious school and harassments as such would only land you in the court. What is the probability that the rapist may have come from our school? Unless you already have a strong lead, please don't show up here unannounced. Now please leave. I have a meeting to attend to."

"But the principal at the Boys College told me your signature is required as well to release the documents."

"You won't have my signature then," the Lady Briggs pronounced with an air of finality. "Get a judge to approve your request. As much as I'd like to solve this case and restore dignity and trust to this school, I will not in the process jeopardize my students' privacy!" The lady stood up and gestured toward the door, and the detective departed, somewhat less ceremoniously than he had arrived. He had full confidence that he could solve the crime, but how was he to solve a crime without proper investigative tools? Was he to sniff out the rapist without proper investigations and interrogations? This was only a wild-goose chase.

Lady Briggs was determined to wait for the police to investigate the matter. There was no amount of rush that would make her give in to Chief Akin's men. It wasn't that she didn't want to help solve the crime; rather she was more interested in maintaining the dignity of her school at all cost.

Chapter 6

It was a balmy Monday morning as the principal of King's Boys College summoned all the students to the assembly ground. The entire school had been stunned by the unfortunate incident which had occurred days ago. No one knew exactly what had happened, but each student told his or her own version, embellishing a little on the way they heard it from others.

The assembly ground was filled with young boys, all in their school uniforms, wondering what was going to be revealed at the assembly. The principal, Professor Dele, a stout, bald-headed man with an over-sized sky-blue suit and cream shirt, walked in with the boarding master. His face was expressionless as he brought out a black ball pen and checked off a square on the agenda from the folder he was carrying.

Professor Dele removed his glasses and folded them into a hard-shell spectacles holder. "Good morning, Gentlemen," he greeted the anxious boys.

"Good morning sir!" the students chorused.

"To say that I am disappointed at the latest development is an understatement," Professor Dele began. "I'm sure you all have heard about the incident at the girls' school a few days ago. There has been an on-going investigation which has interrupted some school events. I assure you that everything will return to normal in due time."

He leaned forward, and spoke earnestly. "If you know anything that might aid this investigation, please do come forward. Let me remind you all that this is a zero tolerance school when it comes to violence in any form. You are also advised not to speak to anyone concerning this matter without the permission of your parents. You may return to your classes now," the principal announced. The students mumbled as they walked away in confusion.

Nedu was embarrassed by his actions, but most of all, he was petrified by what could happen if he ever turned himself in. He kept away from school for days under the pretense that he was ill. He was careful not to give himself away to even his closest friends. He knew it was only a matter of time before the police would have to rest the case; he knew the girl didn't recognize him.

The rural area surrounding the school wasn't equipped with crime solving tools to be able to pin down a criminal. Crime solving was a guessing game with the local detectives, he reasoned.

His mother walked in the house to announce that his father, who lived in the state of Michigan in the United States, had sent for him. She handed him the traveling documents which she had received in the mail. He was excited about the news but was careful not to reveal what he would be running away from. With that, he quietly left the country a rapist.

Two months after the incident, Chief Akin, after an infinite but ineffectual hunt for his daughter's rapist, decided to rest the case. What more could he do? Brenda returned to school, but things went from bad to worse for her. She became the talk of the school. Her roommates referred to her as the girl who was raped. Rita got into a lot of trouble fighting people who spoke ill of her friend. Some even blamed Brenda for being in the location at the first place. Others whispered that there wasn't much hold to this rape story and that her story was practically unbelievable when she couldn't identify the culprit.

One morning, she woke up feeling dizzy with a light headache. She had a sudden urge to vomit, so she ran to the toilet. After throwing up, she noticed a vomit stain on her night gown and pulled some tissue to wipe it off. As she rubbed the tissue on her chest, she felt a sharp pain in her nipples. They looked fuller than before. She couldn't make out the cause of the sudden illness but had a feeling that it could be what she ate the night before. She waited to see if any of her room mates would complain about the same symptoms. She felt weaker by the day and slept all through her classes. The constant urge to vomit continued for days without anyone sharing the same symptoms like she anticipated. She knew it was only a matter of time before Lady Briggs would send her home to get a treatment before returning to school, to avoid infecting everyone else with her illness.

Rita woke her up in the wee hours of the next morning and dragged her to the school yard. She handed her a brownish liquid in a cup to drink. She explained to her that this would eliminate any symptom she was feeling, and would terminate any pregnancy if that was the reason for her symptoms. "You will be thrown out of this school and you will remain a dropout, unless your parents fly you abroad. Worst case, you may spend years at home nurturing a child. Is that what you want?" Rita asked when confronted by Brenda's shocked look.

"What do you mean pregnancy? Who told you I'm pregnant?"

"How I knew isn't the problem right now. The most important thing is getting rid of it. It's obvious, and the girls are already talking. It's just a matter of time before it flies into lady Brigg's sharp ears. So please drink this and get it over with." She commanded Brenda whose eyes widened with horror.

"You mean ev-everyone knows?" Brenda stammered.

"Please drink this before someone finds us here. I paid a lot to have this sent to me here." Brenda drank the content in the cup and grimaced in displeasure. She heard a rumbling sound in her stomach and caught Rita smiling at her as if the remedy had worked instantly. They quietly walked back into their room.

Brenda waited to see if there was going to be any form of bleeding as Rita had proclaimed. Later that day, Lady Briggs sent for Brenda, demanding that she return home at once before she spread any type of illness she may have. The news of the pregnancy had apparently not reached her ears yet.

In a heated argument, Chief Akin's sister demanded that he acquire a UK visa for her son who had been deported from Spain six months ago. He had gotten involved with drug traffickers and been apprehended by the city police. He was arraigned, and the best punishment was to deport him back to Nigeria to languish away indefinitely.

His mother blamed Chief Akin for not supporting her son financially. So that day, she had come to collect some money to send her son back to Europe, but this time to United Kingdom instead of Spain to start his life afresh. He listened as she seethed in his office. She reminded him that he only had a daughter who would someday get married, and that she would never participate in the family will if anything ever happened to him.

In a gesture completely unlike Chief Akin, who usually takes insults in a grave manner, he burst out laughing at his sister's ideas. He hadn't thought about death, or what would happen to his only child if he didn't wake up the next morning. "You speak as if you've forgotten that I was the one who sent him to Spain," he reminded her. I don't know what else you would have me do,"

"He's your nephew and you have to help him," she cried angrily. "You have enough money to send him to heaven if you wanted to. Who else is there for me to go to if not my brother?"

After listening to his sister's desperate rants, he relented. "All right, tell him to see me tomorrow morning so we can discuss his future. Maybe we can discuss getting him married so he would concentrate on his keeping a life together instead thinking only of himself. This will…" he began but was interrupted by his cell phone.

Chief Akin quickly answered the call from his daughter's school. They told him that she was ill and should see a doctor immediately. He gathered his belongings and dashed out of the office.

"What else would make you dash out like this if not your frail daughter?" Bukky snapped as her brother rushed out of the office. Ignoring his sister's further rants, he rushed to his wife's shop and together they drove toward the college. They had driven for five miles when they noticed a lorry speeding in a wrong lane. The driver of the tank lost control with his brakes and diverted to the opposite route. Seeing the Akin's car speeding towards him, the tanker driver slammed on the weak brake and diverted to the middle of the road. He screeched his tires and with a quick turn, released the tank which was filled with crude oil, smashing into the car which was now few feet away. The tanker exploded, releasing a wild inferno. The couple was roasted alive.

Chapter 7

Brenda who was now resting at the school clinic kept glancing at her watch and wondered why her parents hadn't showed up yet. This was the second time they were late to pick her up. She dialed their number several times, but just got the "not available" message. She waited for the whole day without any sign of her parents. "If they were always this unreliable when it comes to visiting her, what would happen when it's graduation?" She pondered.

It was quarter past six in the morning when the overnight security guard knocked on her door to announce that she had an urgent visitor. Was it her parents, or had they sent a driver for her? She walked gently behind the old man and shivered in the chilly weather. She was led to the large waiting room and saw the woman she referred to as "Aunty Bukky" standing, dabbing at her eyes which were red from crying. She had only seen Bukky a few times at their house and had heard stories of how she had advised her brother Chief Akin against marrying Brenda's mother. She only visited them when she needed money from her brother. She was a despicable woman, and whatever had brought her to Brenda's school at such an early hour must be of urgent interest.

"Oh, Brenda *omo mi ooo* – my daughter," the woman wept uncontrollably as she ran to Brenda to hug her. "My dear, the worst has happened. You must come home with me at once. I have explained everything to your boarding mistress." Brenda, still astonished, stood and watched as the woman expressed her pain.

"Go and get your things, we must leave at once!" she commanded.

"But where are my parents?" Brenda demanded, confused.

43

"I will explain everything to you when we get home. This is not the time for questions so hurry up."

Brenda's mind reeled, but she went to her room and dressed for the ride. She followed her aunt to her rickety 1992 Volvo. The car roared out of the quiet school compound that morning, sending dark clouds of smoke in the air.

Brenda's home was filled with guests who were there to pay their last respect to the couple. Some tried to console her and even offered their complimentary card to call them if she ever needed anything. She had been accepting greetings from strangers when her symptoms attacked her again. She was getting some water from the fridge when she collapsed. The men who had come to the wake rushed her to the hospital.

The doctor didn't hesitate to announce to Bukky that Brenda was twelve weeks pregnant. Bukky felt like smothering Brenda who turned her face in shame. She was disappointed because Rita had promised her that the remedy she drank would expel the pregnancy. She hadn't even buried her parents yet and now she learns she is pregnant with no one to guide her.

"I said it! I said it to my younger brother but he didn't listen. His all-so-precious daughter is pregnant. Hei...I wish he was here to witness this." Bukky lamented. "Couldn't you have at least waited for your parents to spend the night in their graves before you rub this abomination to their faces?"

"I did nothing wrong, aunty. I was raped four months ago."

"Raped indeed," her aunt sputtered. "How could you be raped when you were locked up in that expensive girl's school like a bird in a cage? Did your rapist fly in or did you go to meet him? Look, I'm not your friend so you better save your lies for those who are dumb enough to listen to your cheap lies. Because of you, my brother and his lovely wife met their early graves. At your age you still depended on them for even a glass of water. *Oya na,* - Now it has happened. *Aje ni ye* – Evil child." Bukky yelled and stormed out of the ward. Her anger and curses filled the hospital hallway. Nurses and patients wondered what was worrying her.

After the burial of Chief and Mrs. Akin, the family members decided that it would be beneficial for Brenda if she lived with her aunt at least till she turned twenty-one. They also decided that she needed a woman's assistance since she was pregnant. Her aunt saw a better opportunity to inherit her late brother's properties. She decided that it was best to move into his brother's house since her two-bedroom flat she shared with her son in Lagos wasn't conducive to her new status -- someone who would become the director of a multi-million dollar company her brother had left behind.

Bukky grew worse as the days went by and never stopped reminding her niece of how she killed her parents with her bad luck and how she left school in disgrace. Brenda endured all the ill-treatment she received from her aunt but hoped and prayed that God would give her the strength to carry on. She always hoped to return to school someday, but that wouldn't be a topic for Bukky's ears. The doctor advised her to avoid stress as her blood pressure was fluctuating, often very high when she had her pre-natal appointments, but Bukky cared nothing about Brenda's condition.

Nine months into her pregnancy, she had just returned from her routine appointment when she met her cousin, Kunle, lying incautiously on the couch watching pornography. He noticed Brenda walk in so he quickly got up, pulled up his pants, slipped into his slippers and followed her to her room. He quickly shut the door behind him and gave a wicked grin at Brenda who ignored him and lowered herself to the one-sitter couch in her room. "What do you want, Kunle?" she asked wearily.

Kunle didn't respond as he gawked at her lustfully. He gently walked towards her but Brenda tried to escape. He angrily pushed her to the bed behind him and began ripping off her clothes.

"I bet you enjoyed it the first time it happened right?" he taunted as he tried to stop her from fighting him off. He was almost in luck until Bukky, who had returned from the office heard the sound coming from the room downstairs. She dashed into the room and yanked her son away from the pregnant girl. She walked over to Brenda who was sniveling at the corner of the bed, and tried to hide her nakedness while curled up. She glared at her for some seconds and said quietly, with a cold malevolence, "So now you want the god's to lay a curse on my son? This is incest!"

"He tried to rape me, you saw it…" Brenda defended.

"Everyone is out to rape you. You've established that all right. Now get your nauseating self together, and leave my house!" she barked. Brenda hoped Bukky was just shocked and being overly dramatic, but Brenda was the shocked one when Bukky shoved her out of the house to the rainy cold night.

Chapter 8

Edna had spent the last thirty minutes at work trying to calm a customer who was threatening to blow up the company where she worked. The customer had claimed that he forgot a portfolio containing some money at the office the last time he visited. He reported it to the manager who attempted to convince him of the honesty of his employees, telling him that they wouldn't have hesitated to report the item had they found it. The discontented customer felt that it was either that another customer had taken the portfolio or that one of the employee was concealing it.

Unfortunately, the only person whom he had his eyes on was Edna. She was there the day the portfolio disappeared. Edna on the other hand, knew nothing about the portfolio. His ranting and raving emptied the lobby of other customers. One would think he was about to blow the whole place up. The man was escorted out by the security men. It was an arduous day for Edna who left the office horrified, and hoped not to see the man again. As she sped on the highway, she kept replaying the incident over and over in her head.

She decided that it was better that she get off the highway and take the back road. If indeed the man was following her, she would see people to run to for help. As she slowed down and turned to the ramp exit which was a longer route to her street, she realized she needed some fuel for her generator at home. The national electric power supply had been undergoing some reconstruction, so this affected the power supply in the whole town. So people had to use generators. She stopped by the gas station and filled a plastic keg she had in her trunk and drove off. The heavy downpour prevented her from seeing the road clearly as she galloped through the nasty pot holes on the road. She came to a complete halt when she noticed a pregnant girl soaking wet, crossing the street. She first honked loud and cursed at the girl who seem not have noticed the car, but when she realized that she was pregnant and soaking wet from the rain, she pulled over and got out of the car. She ran to the girl who was shivering and frightened. Edna spoke to her a couple of times, but the girl didn't respond. She gently helped her to her feet and led her to the passenger side of her car. Edna couldn't concentrate in her driving as she kept glancing at the pregnant girl sited beside her. She decided it was best to rush her to the hospital because the girl seemed to be in shock. She kept wondering what could have caused the girl's state of mind. The girl was so thin, despite her obviously late pregnancy, that Edna surmised the girl had not eaten anything for days.

Eight hours after they arrived at the hospital, the doctor came to announce to Edna who had been roaming in the wide corridor of the hospital that the girl whom she had brought in earlier just delivered a set of twins, a boy and a girl. Edna danced around the hospital as if it was her own daughter that delivered. She hugged all the nurses that walked her way. She sang praises and whistled her way to the hospital ward where Brenda lay asleep.

She peered at the infant bed beside her where the twins were laying. She gently picked up the baby girl, rubbed her thumb on her cheeks and smiled. She brought her face closer as the infant tickled her chin with her tight little fist. She then gently pulled the baby boy's foot playfully and laughed when the infant retracted his tiny foot. She clasped her hands together in excitement as if she was offered an unexpected gift. Her joy was so complete that she forgot her plans about finding Brenda's family once she was hospitalized.

She was startled when Brenda woke up and began to scream. Brenda didn't recognize the woman who was holding her baby. She ogled Edna and shifted her gaze to the baby she was holding, quickly springing out of the bed in uncertainty. Edna quickly put the baby down and went to console her. She walked gently to her and placed her arm around her neck.

"It's alright my dear. I'm not here to harm you. My name is Edna. I was the one who brought you here last night. Would you like me to call any of your family members now, perhaps, your husband? He must be looking for you now."

Brenda shook her head vigorously.

"Then maybe you'd like to tell me your name?" Edna queried, mystified at the girl's reaction.

"Brenda....Brenda Akin," she pronounced. "Are you married?"

Brenda shook her head and lowered her eyes in shame.

"Forgive my curiosity but I just want to understand. You've been here for hours now and no one has come to look for you. If there's any way I can help..."the woman pleaded, squeezing her shoulder, as she fixated her eyes on the twins who gently wiggled on the bed.

Brenda had never felt so much love in her life as the first time she stared at her twins. They looked so fragile that she feared picking them up would be dangerous. The small innocent faces stared right into her eyes and the boy smiled shyly and cooed. Those smiles made her feel like there was nothing to worry about. She smiled back as if nothing had been wrong with her life. After some time of watching the babies play, she jealously picked the baby boy up and placed him comfortably in her wide lap. She placed all her life experiences behind the moment she held her babies. She knew it was the establishment of a new life for her.

Edna returned to the hospital the next day immediately after work with cheerful balloons and a plate of food. The balloons were given to her by some of her colleagues at work with whom she unexpectedly shared the story. She had told them that Brenda was her niece, and they shared the woman's joy.

She also had a small bag with some clothes in it for the babies and their mother. She hung the balloons happily and went to see the twins again. She chuckled and turned to their mother. Brenda who had been staring at her babies all day without thinking of food eagerly grabbed the plate of food as Edna attended to the twins. The aroma of the fresh cat fish pepper soup with assorted beef intestines filled the room. It was the type of soup that was served to nursing mothers as well. She hadn't smelt such a well prepared meal since her parents died. She quickly wolfed down the food and gulped down glasses of chilled bottled water to tame the heat from the heavily spiced food.

"Have you chosen names for them yet?" Edna asked eagerly.

"No, I'm still thinking about what to call them. I should have thought about that before their due date." Brenda responded innocently.

"I've been thinking of names," Edna responded. "Why don't we call them Richard and Rachelle? I always wanted twins when I was young, and I think they are lovely names for a boy and a girl."

Brenda was silent as she thought about the names.

"Look Brenda, I've been observing you for days now, and it seems there's something you do not want to share. That's fine by me, but I'd like to know that I can trust you? See me as your friend if not family. There's nothing you will tell me that will change my feelings towards you and your children. If you are not ready to discuss what happened to you the night I found you, then at least tell me how to reach your family. They must be worried sick."

"Yes..." Brenda muttered, avoiding the other question.

"What have you been thinking?" Edna gently prodded. "Do you need a place to stay? The doctor told me you are free to leave anytime you wish."

Brenda was still quiet. She hadn't thought about her next move if she ever left the hospital.

"Would you like to stay at my place until you decide your next move?" Edna asked, staring at Brenda who was still trying to quench the heat in her mouth. She didn't look at the woman but picked her nails. The innocence which Brenda had been robbed of returned in a simple gesture from a good woman.

Edna realized that there were probably lots to tell from the look on the girl's face. Brenda ran to hug her. She had been careful not to mention that she had an aunt so Edna wouldn't insist on contacting her. Brenda had already decided that she would sleep in the dump before she returned to Aunt Bukky. She realized she really had no choice; it was either stay with this kind stranger and watch the future unfold, or be on the street, maybe somewhere in an unwed mothers' home. If it was only for herself, she would have had a difficult decision. But she didn't want her children to suffer. She looked at Edna with gleeful eyes. Brenda was discharged from the hospital, and Edna paid the bills and took her home.

Chapter 9

Brenda was indebted to Edna who took care of her and her children like her own. Edna would rush home early from work just to take the children to the play parlor and even to the park to play with other children. She played the loving grandma role perfectly. After six months, she felt it was time to open up to Edna who had been unwearied with her. She felt guilty for not telling the woman her story, but how was she to relive her past without thinking of the appalling death of her parents and the life changing experience that brought her these two children.

Edna sniffed as Brenda told her dreadful life story. She caught herself crying so many times as she listened. She gave a long stare at Brenda, got up and hugged her.

"How could you allow this to eat you up till now?" Edna inquired. "Don't you know that experiences like this will alter your future and hurt your future husband? I am deeply sorry that you had to go through all this. You are safe now my dear. May the souls of your parents rest in peace. Come, I have something to show you," she said, leading Brenda to her bedroom. There, Edna bent under her bed and brought out a big photo album of her and her family. She pointed at each picture in the album.

"Look here," she said, reminiscing. "That's my first husband. I married him when I was thirteen years old. My father was very poor and struggled to feed me and my seven siblings. That's my mother holding me with my siblings. My father took to drinking after he lost his night watchman's job on a small plantation. He met a forty-five year old farmer from another village who promised to loan him some money, and in return he asked for me in marriage. My father agreed without even consulting my mother.

"I was married away to this man," she said, without pausing for breath, "and my father used the money for a bicycle and a quarter plot of farmland with vegetables. I was the fourth and youngest wife to this man. He raped me every night, and even when I got pregnant, he didn't stop. He would drink and slap me around as he wished. I had my first miscarriage at fifteen. When my mother heard the news, she came to take me home, but the man drove her away and warned her never to return.

"My father came to plead with him to allow him take me home but he insisted that since I was his legal wife, no one had any right to take me away from him for even a second. And if my father wished to have me back then he should return the sixteen tubers of yam he collected from him and the quarter plot of land, including the bicycle. My father couldn't provide all these because, by then, he had gambled everything away.

"The war broke out from the south before it hit us," she continued. "When the soldiers invaded my father's village, my mum and siblings were killed. The man didn't even allow me to see their graves. When the war was called off, I escaped from this man's house one night while he was away for his usual drinking. I ran for days. I hid in the bush from the youths my husband had sent to look for me.

"Look here that is Madu, the one I refer to as my real husband," she said, pointing at another photo. "We met in the restaurant where I waited tables. He came there with his friends on his birthday, and our eyes met. It is what you young people call 'love at first sight.' He came back the next day to look for me. We began seeing each other. He was from a very rich family so he made me go back to school. We got married four years after we met. This is my first son Edward, and his younger brother Martin. He likes to be called Edward" She pointed again at another picture in grey. "I took this picture on his fourth birthday." She rubbed the surface of the picture with tenderness.

"They look so much like their father. He recently traveled to the U.S to complete his studies. He was becoming a bit of a headache here. Teenagers are tough you know," Edna narrated to Brenda who was shocked at what she heard.

"How," Brenda wondered, "could someone go through so much pain and still remain strong and happy?"

"So how long has your husband been in the states? Does he ever return?" Brenda asked quietly.

"He's been there for ten years now, and he won't be returning any time soon. We are divorced now."

"Why? What went wrong?" Brenda asked, incredulously.

"Nothing went wrong. Well, I went wrong. Do you now see the reason why I was sad earlier when you told me your story? This type of experience will only hurt you and the men you come in contact with. It may be different for some, but you will always see men as predators. That was what happened to me. I can't really explain it, but I grew more uncomfortable around him after I had my second son Martin.

"You need to let go of all your hatred for those who have hurt you in the past," Edna pronounced. "That is the only way forward, my dear. He was patient, but my irritability grew worse. We decided it was best if we stayed apart. He was so heartbroken that he relocated to the states. We still communicate, but I didn't want to continue hurting him."

Edna continued showing her the faces in the photos without noticing Brenda's astonished eyes. "You have to make peace with yourself and with whatever is causing you pain before you can accommodate others," Edna advised.

Brenda soon began attending evening classes at a private school in town. She would wait for Edna to return from work to babysit the children while she went to school. She sat for her final year examination and passed very well. She got admitted into a state University south of town. That was where she met Toni.

Toni was a mixture of a Nigerian and American parents. Her parents relocated to Nigeria from America, so they decided to keep her close, being the only child. She and Brenda had met one afternoon after classes while Brenda was waiting for the bus to get back home. Toni saw her standing in the lonely street and pulled over before her.

"Hello, do you need a ride?,"?" Toni asked, solicitously.

Brenda glanced at her and walked inches away from the car.

"I am talking to you," Toni called out. "You may not find a bus here on time, or you might even spend another half hour waiting. Why don't you get in and let me drop you somewhere."

"Do I know you?" Brenda asked.

"We haven't met, really, but I think I saw you in my philosophy class this afternoon?" Toni responded.

Brenda heard that and relaxed a bit. She opened the door of the car and got into the passenger seat. She took time to glance around the interior of the comfy Honda Civic, and toward the driver, a light skinned girl with dark curly hair, and a round face with thick eye brows and round eyes.

"I'm Brenda," she said at last.

"Toni. So where are you headed to?"

55

"15 Anolue Crescent near the roundabout before exit 31," Brenda recited.

"I know the place. My boyfriend's family lives there as well."

"Cool," Brenda smiled, adjusting her seat as the car sped. There was an awkward silence in the car as they drove. Soon the car arrived in front of her house. Brenda turned to Toni who smiled at her.

"Thanks a lot. You saved my day."

"Please don't mention it. Do you have classes tomorrow?" Toni inquired.

"Yes, I have a class at 10."

"Oh that's great. I have a class at 11:20 tomorrow. If you'd like, I could give you a ride," Toni offered.

"But your class is later than mine. Won't you get bored waiting for it?"

"I can always hang around the school and study," Toni answered. "Trust me the time will go by quickly. Besides, it's tough getting a bus in the morning to get to school. I know they always stop at Ogba junction, and then you have to wait for another bus to get to the campus. I'll be here tomorrow at 9:15, all right?" she asked.

"Oh, thank you," Brenda smiled and stepped out of the car. She stood and waited for Toni to drive off and waved to her. The she turned and entered the compound.

Brenda woke up at 7 and hurried to the shower as usual. She dressed up, and went into her children's room to get them ready. She went to the kitchen to prepare breakfast for them so that Edna could drop them off at the day care on her way to work. This had been their routine for years now. Brenda continued to glance at the clock since she was expecting Toni soon.

She plugged in the electric kettle and brought out some eggs from the fridge. She cracked a few, added some spices, and whisked them together. She lighted a match on the burner and placed a frying pan on it. She poured the eggs in the pan and watched them fry. She began setting the table and then noticed Richard chewing his shoe. She rushed over to him, snatched the shoe, and forced it back on his foot.

"Don't do that again," she warned and rushed back to the kitchen. She began dishing out the eggs and pouring hot water in their tea cups. She went up to the stairs to announce to Edna that breakfast was ready. She ran back downstairs to feed her children and ate too. Edna joined them at the dining table and ate as well; then she walked out with the kids.

Brenda breathed a sigh of relief knowing that the hustle for that morning was over. She cleaned up the table and went to her room to get her bag before Toni arrived. Just as she expected, Toni arrived on time and they drove off.

Toni became a regular caller at Brenda's house. She visited her on weekends and they studied together or sometimes went shopping. They became each other's confidantes in their time of need so that even Edna couldn't understand the attachment.

On the last day of their finals, Toni decided to take her friend to the fast food restaurant on the school campus. As they walked to their seats with the tray of food and drinks, Toni's cell phone rang. Brenda placed her tray on the round glass table, adjusted the belt of her jeans, and sipped her orange juice with a straw. She waited for Toni to finish her call.

Toni smiled and winked at her patient friend. Then she let out a loud, "Yes!" stunning other customers so that they turned to stare. She pinched Brenda's hand and smiled.

"I am traveling to United states!" she crowed.

"What?" Brenda queried, a crushed look shadowing her face.

"I said I'm traveling back to the states. You remember I told you about Ken, my fiancé who traveled to UK years back and began playing football? He just got a contract to play in the US, and now he wants us to get married," Toni explained excitedly.

"Wow!! That's good news," Brenda said, cheerfully, hiding her dismay from her elated fried. "So when are you traveling, or should I say, when are you guys getting married?"

"He said he will be home this month to see my parents before we leave together. He wants a church wedding in the US so all his friends can attend. The traditional wedding will be held here of course."

"I guess I can't attend my best friend's wedding then," Brenda replied.

"Come on, it's not like that," Toni coaxed. "You must attend; if not I won't get married," she demonstrated playfully.

"If you hold the wedding in Nigeria, then I'll attend. I don't have a visa and I'm sure it may not be ready by the time your wedding comes, even if I apply for one now."

"Either way, we will work something out. I will ask Ken to find out more about getting you a Visa" Toni assured her.

The problem with Brenda wasn't that she didn't want her friend to be happy, but that she knew she was going to be lonely again when Toni left. She tried to hide her worries from her overly excited friend as they ate and chatted further.

"That reminds me, you told me once that your foster mother has two sons who live abroad, have you met them?" Toni inquired as she bite into her beef patty. "No I haven't. I've only seen their photos. I hope to someday.

Their mother has been very kind to me and I can't thank them enough."

"What do they look like?" Toni asked.

"Handsome, handsome, handsome," Brenda responded.

"Really? I'm sure you'll have to choose when they return."

"They are my brothers," Brenda said. "I can only admire their looks, not drool all over them."

"Yeah, right. They are not your brothers, you just happen to live with their mother. One can only imagine what would happen with all that *Konji* – those sexual urges locked up inside you. I wish I had a brother; I would have pleaded with him to help you out. It may take days to relieve you, you know," Toni teased and laughed.

Brenda kicked her friend under the table.

"But it's true *na*," Toni said. "You haven't been with a man for years and I wonder what will happen when your so-called brothers walk around in their boxers, or shirtless....mmmmhmmm," Toni continued.

"You know damn well that being with a man is the least of my priorities now," Brenda said, defensively. "I don't want anyone. I am happy being single. My children bring me so much joy that I can't have any other."

"But you haven't answered me; what will you do if they walk around shirtless baring all those foreign goodies before you?" Toni asked.

"I'll call you to come and help me, silly," Brenda retorted.

"Don't worry, when you meet the right man, you will sing a different tune." Toni assured.

Brenda smiled and dipped her fork into the roasted chicken on her plate and took a bite.

Burning Wind

After Toni's traditional wedding, she and her husband left for the US. Brenda was unhappy because the visiting visa her friend's fiancé applied for her didn't arrive until two months after the wedding, so she couldn't attend her church wedding. Brenda returned to her boring and silent life, and spoke with her friend on the phone all the time. She would listen as Toni described Ken's mansion to her and told her beautiful stories of America. They would gossip and advise each other every now and then.

Chapter 10

Seven years had passed by. Bukky who had been managing the late Chief Johnson's company, with her lust for money and without proper training, quickly squandered everything her brother had worked for. All the best employees, who had helped Chief Akin manage the company efficiently, all left.

Bukky began selling off the properties and turned to gambling to try to increase her ever-dwindling resources. She spent money on younger men who in turn pleased her sexually. Most of them ripped her off a lot of money, and her son was no exception. He used the house for collateral while he gambled and partied as much as he could. The final straw came when the company was liquidated by the bank.

Bukky and her son were soon thrown into the streets, where they faced a huge hardship. Tunde, out of desperation to bounce back to wealth joined his group of friends for a bank robbery one Saturday afternoon at a local bank. It was the bank where Edna worked, but luckily she wasn't there that day because she stayed behind to watch the children while Brenda went to complete her school registration. They stole all they could from the bank safe but faced the police on their way out. They exchanged gun fire with the police squad, and all his friends were gunned down. Tunde was hit in the knee, and was quickly arrested with no bail. Out of shame, Bukky relocated to the village.

Edna announced to Brenda one day that her sons would be returning in three days time. Brenda had looked forward to meeting Edna's sons for the past seven years. They had taken her as a member of the family and often sent gifts to her children. Edna, beyond excited, couldn't wait to see her sons once again. On the day of their arrival, Edna and Brenda cooked and cleaned the entire house. Brenda stayed behind with the twins while Edna drove to the airport. After setting the table, she picked up her phone and dialed Toni's number, but it went straight to voice mail. She sighed and looked at clock, realizing it was midnight in US. She wanted to chat a bit with her friend before the family arrived.

An hour later, the door burst open to the sound of hoarse laughter and luggage wheels. Suddenly in the front hallway stood two tall and handsome men. The twins grabbed on to Edna's oldest son Edward, as they entered the house, seemingly mesmerized by him. Edward couldn't stop staring at Rachelle. She was eight years old but already developed the body of a teenager. He quickly guided them both to the living room where Brenda sat, giggling in self-conscious delight. She smoothed her sky-blue blue skirt, proffering her hand for a shake.

"You must be Brenda," he said quietly with his deep, sonorous voice. "Nice to finally meet you. I must say you look positively scrumptious in person." He smiled, revealing row of perfect, white teeth.

He smelled of Ralph Lauren sport cologne as Brenda drew closer to him. She melted as she gently placed her hand on his. "Welcome home," she said, gracefully, beaming a smile as she gazed at his thin lips.

Martin walked in on them staring at each other. "Brenda! Come here," he commanded playfully and hugged Brenda, lifting her off the ground.

"Damn!" Martin mocked, playfully. "Mum, you didn't tell us that you had the most beautiful girl in your house. I'm hurt, Ma," he said, calling for Edna who was still outside, as he stared at Brenda.

The family burst into laughter. Martin has always been the loudest and most playful one in the family, while his older brother was the quiet type. Brenda was overwhelmed by the attention these men paid her and her children, and for the first time, she felt she really belonged to a family. She knew their stay would be a fun one.

The door opened as Edna, looking annoyed, walked in with a girl who appeared to be the same age as Brenda. The girl walked into the house dragging her luggage. Edna regained her composure and beckoned everyone to the dining table. Brenda stared at their faces and sensed that something had happened while she was exchanging pleasantries with the men inside.

"Brenda, I'd like you to meet Efe, Edward's fiancée," Edna said in a quiet, controlled voice. She glared at her son who quickly turned his face to the window. Edna was rendered utterly perplexed since her son had not mentioned his engagement to her before now, and it irritated her though she wasn't sure why.

Brenda smiled at Efe, but her smile was returned with a glower. Brenda's smile quickly disappeared. She turned to Martin who had been staring at her hips since he sat down to the table. The family was quiet as they ate.

"So Brenda how long have you been here?" Efe broke the silence, sipping her drink.

"I've been here for years now. I lost count because Mama has been kind to me and my children." Brenda cheerfully responded. Edna glared at Efe, seemingly irritated by the question. Who is she to ask questions about anything in her house?

"What's wrong with my question, or are the kids not going to find out what their father did?" Efe asked, sensing Edna's facial expression.

"What business of yours is it to find out how long she's been here?" Edna asked angrilyinterrupted. Efe withdrew and gulped down her glass of orange juice.

"What about their father?" Efe continued her questions pointing at Brenda's children. "Were you married?" Efe continued to ask Brenda.

Edna wasn't enjoying the conversation at all. Brenda didn't have an answer for the last two questions so she simply left the table. The men couldn't help but wonder why Edna and Brenda seemed so tense.

Edna glanced around the table in anger and went after her. "My daughter, please stop.! Do not let that roach ruin your mood this night. She's always been an attention seeker so please don't let her get to you."

"Mama, I've already accepted my fate but the last thing I need is someone to remind me of it, even in the presence of these children." Brenda sobbed. "I know my dear. I apologize again. You see, that was the problem before I came into the house. I had to sit in the car with her for a little chat. I told her that we have children in the house and that she mustn't smoke anywhere in this compound. I don't know why Edward brought her here."

"She smokes?"

"Yes she does. She can finish two packs in a day. I don't know what exactly he saw in this girl," Edna said.

"Did she agree not to smoke in this house?" Brenda wanted to know.

"I doubt it because of the response she gave to me. She said she will think about it. Well it's my house and I will not allow her to disobey my rules. The most annoying part of it is that this girl has been the reason why I sent him to that Boy's school. He was in a better school in Senegal and was discharged in one year. I don't know exactly how she came to the picture, but she is a bad influence. So, my daughter, please don't mind her, okay?" Edna consoled her as she rubbed her back gently.

Brenda breathed a sigh of relief and returned to the dining table. Everyone ate in silence. After the meal, Edna helped Brenda clean up from the meal while Efe stormed to Edward's room. Martin lifted a sleeping Richard from the couch and moved toward his room. Edward guided a sleepy Rachelle to her room, and tucked her in, sitting at the edge of the bed, just staring at her and caressing her face. He felt so strange. This child bore a marked resemblance to him. It was like looking into his own face as a child.

After cleaning the kitchen, Brenda went to check on her kids before retiring to bed. Edward was reading to Rachelle. She was reminded of how her father used to read to her every night. She stood at the door unnoticed as he gently stood up, turned off the light and turned around to find Brenda standing at the door gaping at him.

"I hope they didn't wear you out? They can be so demanding at times," she whispered. "You seem like one who loves children a lot." She continued.

"Shhhh....don't wake her," he replied.

"Thank you."

"You needn't thank me," he whispered. "After all I'm their 'uncle'. They are truly adorable. You did a good job." He replied as he stared at Brenda's eyes, and winked.

"I couldn't have done it without your lovely mother." Brenda reminded him.

"Good night," he concluded, smiling.

She replied with a good night and stared after him as he turned into the corridor and walked into his bedroom. She returned her gaze to the dark room where her daughter was sleeping and gently shut the door. She brushed the flour from her apron and went into her son's room to check on him as well. Satisfied, she went to her own room to sleep.

Edward developed an attraction towards the twins that no one could fathom. His fiancé could not hide her jealousy.

Chapter 11

Every morning was awkward now as everyone went around bumping into each other and exchanging "sorry" as if it was the order of the day, and today was no exception. The children were already awake and running around the large hallway that led to the living room, playing. Their loud footsteps awoke the entire household.

Martin was the first to appear in the kitchen in his boxers and white tee-shirt. This exposed his hairy long, slender legs and thick calves. He walked to the fridge and grabbed a bottle of water, sucking on it for some time. He grabbed an orange and returned to his room. Efe walked up to Brenda in the kitchen with a stern look as she sipped a cup of hot chocolate.

"Girl talk," she began.

"Good morning," Brenda greeted happily, relieved that Efe was speaking to her.

"I'm guessing you haven't felt a need for a man ever since Aunt Edna brought you and your children here. Anyway, I see the way you and my man have been sharing glances. You better not have anything up your sleeve, *gurl.* I'll be watching--from a corner," Efe threatened, ignoring Brenda's greeting and walking away with a sly smirk on her face.

Brenda stood there speechless watching Efe climb the stairs, wiggling her hips. Brenda's attention was drawn to her hidden emotions towards the man she was being warned about. It was becoming obvious to her that she had fallen for this man in less than a day. However, the stern warning of Efe reminded her to tread cautiously. She sighed and went to the kitchen to prepare breakfast. Erotic thoughts of Edward could not escape her mind. She hadn't been with a man in years but the moment she set her eyes on him, she knew it was only a matter of time before she threw herself on him.

Edward wasn't making things easier for her. He would sneak in on her in the kitchen, read her a poem he had written and ask for her opinion. She found most of his poems very romantic but would respond professionally as expected. His presence was beginning to torture her emotionally. She cherished every moment he spent chatting with her. Most importantly, he showered her kids with lots of love. Soon her cell phone rang and when she saw the caller ID, she happily answered the call and ran into her room.

"Hey girl, sorry I didn't return your call," Toni's voice came across the ocean. "I've been busy all week. I saw your missed call three days ago. Have they arrived?"

"Yes they have. Oh my God, they are so fine."

"I told you, but you argued. So who is making you blush today?" "

"I'm not blushing," Brenda defended as she walked towards the mirror on her bedroom wall. She stared at herself talking on the phone. There, she realized her mood was lighter that morning.

"You are still in denial my friend. Okay, give me the gist then, what's up?"

"They are really nice to my kids but the elder son came back with a girlfriend attached."

"Are you serious?" Toni interrupted.

"Honestly, I think I'm falling for him."

"Falling for who? The older one or the younger one?"

"The older one, of course. You should see his eyes and his body," Brenda described as she drew a shapeless image on the mirror.

"Does he like you?"

"I don't know. I think he does. The way he looks at me and reads his poems to me." "He's a poet?" Toni asked.

"Not really. He does it for fun and just reads them to me."

"And his girlfriend?" Toni queried further.

"She's there. She even threatened me this morning if I so much as look at him."

"Be careful my friend. I have to run now. Give me more tomorrow, okay? Take care now, bye."

"Bye," Brenda replied and hung up. She smiled and continued to stare at the mirror. She fixed her hair and left the room.

On the other hand, Martin who had noticed the way Edward and Brenda were becoming close also made his intentions known. Since his older brother was already engaged, he felt whatever was left in the pot was reserved for him.

One afternoon, he took Brenda out on a date for Cantonese cuisine near the sea side. They ate and laughed for a long time as he told her his experiences while in the U.S.

She laughed at all his jokes, and Martin had a feeling that if he continued to make her laugh, she might end up falling in love with him. But Brenda knew that Martin was only as good as his jokes. He took her on a boat ride after their lunch and went to the cinema.

They returned home later at night to find Edward with Richard leaning on him. They had dozed off in the living room. She was moved by what she saw. She gently eased Richard off Edward's lap. He had been reading them a story as he waited for her to return, not knowing she was on a date with Martin. When he felt Richard's weight off his chest, he looked up and saw Brenda standing over him with a sympathetic look on her face. He turned to see his brother, Martin, standing beside Brenda and returned his gaze to her saying, "They waited up for you. Next time, please remember to call and find out who is home with them." Then he got up and walked away.

Edward wasn't happy seeing Brenda and his brother together. Brenda said nothing but went to lay Richard in his room. She kept awake thinking about what Edward said and how he said it. Could it be he was worried or jealous about where she had been with his brother, she wondered. But she dozed off moments later.

Efe had just returned from her home town where she had gone to visit her family. When she returned after a week and noticed the friendship between Brenda and Edward had grown deeper, she was disgruntled at the sudden change in her relationship due to the swift attraction her man had developed overnight for this girl. She had to fight for her right, so she decided it was time to go back to Chicago. She felt that Edward loved her very well and had always listened to her wishes. She planned on traveling back to Chicago with Edward before she lost him forever.

She had the discussion scenario already rehearsed in her mind as she presented her case before Edward who was talking with his lawyer in the parlor on a cold afternoon. She barged in on him and demanded he follow her immediately for a chat. The man, who had grown unconcerned with the lady he proposed to marry, waved her off as he was deep into the conversation with his lawyer.

"Edward, I need to talk to you right now," she barked. He glanced at her and, seeing the seriousness in her face, he gently excused himself from his lawyer, and led her into the corridor.

"What is it that can't wait till my meeting is over? I've warned you several times about your attitude toward people. You didn't even speak to the man sitting there. What is wrong with you?"

"I'm going back to the states in two days," she blurted, ignoring his questions.

"Good! Call me when you get there," he retorted sarcastically.

"We are going back together, Edward."

"I'm not ready to leave yet. In fact I think I'm staying here for a while. I see a lot of potential to diversify my investments here. The man I'm talking to has helped me investigate fast rising businesses and investments here. From what he has shown me, I think I would be hitting a gold mine if I ever decided to settle here.

"You can go ahead without me," he continued, "and I'll keep you updated. I'm sorry," he said. "I have to go back to the meeting now. This gentleman and I have a lot to sort out."

He pecked her on the cheek, squeezed her shoulder gently and walked away leaving her standing in the corridor with her mouth wide open. She managed to mutter his name but lost courage. She turned her attention to Brenda who was helping her children with their homework in the den. She fumed at Brenda who hadn't heard the conversation.

Efe didn't need a soothsayer to interpret Edward's actions. She knew she was slowly losing him, and that he wasn't in love with her anymore. Her impulse was to discuss it with her mother-in-law-to-be, but Efe was discouraged by Edna's attitude toward her. She knew that the only reason she was still in this house was because Edward had pleaded with his mother to forgive her and consider her as her future daughter-in-law. However, Efe's attitude hadn't gained her much balance in the house. It was obvious that no one liked her, and announcing her departure wouldn't change anything--rather it might call for a celebration.

Realizing her position, Efe quickly packed her belongings and left without informing either Edna or her fiancé. She dragged her luggage jaggedly along the black-top road and hailed a cab which drove her to the airport.

After two dates with Martin, Brenda realized there was something missing; in as much as she enjoyed his jokes and jovial ways of treating her, she didn't have any feelings for him. She often imagined being on a date with his brother instead. She thought about a way to spell it out to him without hurting his feelings. He was clearly more interested in her than she was in him. He had been there as a distraction when Efe accused her of casting a lustful eye on Edward. She hoped going out with his brother would dissolve her feelings for him, but it only made them stronger. But now that Efe was gone, there may be a chance for her. With that, she thought about uncomplicated ways to break loose of Martin.

Valentine's Day was fast approaching and Hamattan season was in its full vigor. People could barely walk out of their homes without having to inhale the dust that rose from passing vehicles. The red dust which turned to thick and slippery mud in the rainy season covered the paved side of the road. It was not a good day to appear in white clothing. However, the chilly weather made people stay indoors, and romance cropped up at all angles.

That afternoon, Brenda was whistling away as she vigorously rubbed baby oil into her skin when she heard a knock on the door. With a towel loosely tied round her waist, she opened the door and hid behind it, popping her head out to inquire what the person wanted. It was her son Richard standing there with a smile on his face as he handed a bouquet of roses to her.

"Will you like to go out on a date with me, will you be my Val?" he mumbled innocently as he spelled out the overly rehearsed lines. At first she was shocked by the way her son spoke to her, and then wondered who must have put him up to it. She saw a man in him already and she knew he would definitely sweep a woman off her feet if he continued to speak like that. She burst into laughter as the young boy searched her face for clues.

"Of course baby, I'll be your Val," she replied still giggling. The boy boastfully walked away with an air of accomplishment. She was still staring at the roses when Edward appeared from the hallway with a smile on his face. She was so shocked to see him standing in front of her that she lost her composure and the small towel she had covered herself with dropped to the floor like a theatre drape exposing her nakedness. Mortified, she quickly clutched her private area with the bouquet and covered her boobs with the other arm with a discomfited look on her face. Edward stood there, nonplussed by the incident and quickly turned away, apologizing. What was supposed to be a romantic invitation turned out to be an imaginative one. Edward walked down the hall smiling to himself and turned back for the second time to see if she was still watching him.

The thought of the incident made Brenda chuckle every time she remembered it, despite the fact that she was still mortified by it. She hadn't planned for their romance to begin that way either. She obsessed, wishing she hadn't humiliated herself the way she did before him.

For days, she avoided him and often found excuses to steer clear of the table at mealtime. Moreover, the way he looked at her when she lied to his mother about not wanting to eat together, made her realize that he knew what she as thinking.

She was itching to hear what he had to say in response to the incident. Later that night, she summoned courage to visit him in his room. She wanted to talk to him about the way she felt towards him. Her feelings had become a slow torture to her, and she wanted him to hear it. It was already eleven forty-five and everyone else had retired for the evening, so she felt it was the perfect time to see him. She didn't want Edna to think wrongly about her.

She slipped into her night gown, sprayed a fruity mist on her body and walked gently down the hallway so as not to alert Martin whose room was two doors away from his brother's. She gently opened the door and sneaked into the dark room where Edward was lying. She turned on the lamp beside his bed and tapped him on the shoulder. He rolled over and woke up to see Brenda gleaming. He rubbed his eyes so as to see her clearly. She had a seductive smile on her face that left him fully awake.

He smiled back, realizing that asking her why she had come to his room would be a totally stupid question. Amazed, he sat up in bed, dragging her close to his chest and kissing her gently on the lips. He stared deep into her glistening eyes that looked as though tears were about to roll out of them. She was weak in his arms and had forgotten the main reason she had paid him that impromptu visit. As much as she wanted to talk to him first, she didn't want to distract him with a chat.

He moved her dark long hair away from her slender neck and gently kissed it. His hand traveled down to the sleeve of her night gown and slipped it away from her shoulders. He then lowered to suck on the inviting stiffened nipples before him. He returned to kissing her on the lips fully and deeply. She moaned at every touch and moved against him. She was now fully lying on her back as Edward gained full control of her curvy body.

Burning Wind

He kissed every part of her as she moaned loudly. Careful not to awake the family with her moaning, he slipped from the bed a moment, inserting the CD that was lying on the table without looking at it. The slow tune of Seal, "I'm Your Man," filled the room. He lowered the volume, and the music sent a wave of pleasure between the two.

He pulled off the sleeveless undershirt he was wearing, exposing his ripped abs and tight arms. She had never seen him half naked, and she became even more excited. He crawled back into the bed and turned her to her stomach, caressing her back, slowing his moves when he reached the contours of her ass. She twisted her neck back and forth gently with her eyes shut. She felt goose bumps all over her skin. He mounted her and began moving gently. Her gentle moans filled the room. He stopped to kiss her on the lips to stop her loud moans. He increased his pace as she dug her nails into his flesh. He slowed and hugged her sweaty body and rolled her over to sit on top of him. She began moving her hips with him inside her, gently. He grabbed her hips tightly as if to decrease the tempo, and she rode him tirelessly. The long and steamy love making ended ceremoniously as they held each other tightly and gasped for breath. The second time seemed better and longer than the first. At last she slept, her head on his chest.

Chapter 12

The morning had passed Brenda by, and for the first time in eight years, she had slept till eleven a.m. Alarmed, she jumped out of bed and realized she was still in Edward's room, but he was not. She didn't want anyone to see her sneaking out of his room, so she gently opened the door and crept out quietly, running to her own room. She bolted the door and panted heavily. She slumped on her bed and stared at the ceiling. She thought about the incident of last night and a gentle smile formed on her lips.

She officially went on a date with him the next day, not minding what his brother would say. She knew she was very much in love with him and wanted to be alone with him. Unlike a date with Martin which was filled with lots of laughter and fun places, she spent most of the evening kissing and hugging Edward.

They took a walk on the beach as the sun was setting. They held hands and walked as they chatted. Brenda felt complete as a woman for the first time in her life. She hadn't wished for her life to turn out this way, but if that was how her God wanted it then she was in the right company. Edward was everything she wanted in a man. He turned out to be very loving, caring and a friend to her. In as much as Edna told her that she did not explain her life details to her sons, it was left for her to tell the story if she pleased.

As they walked in the park one evening, he began asking her, "that night during dinner, you seemed upset when Efe mentioned something aboutut your children's father? " Brenda had known that the question would surface one day, but she wasn't prepared to discuss it. She tried to change the topic, but Edward wouldn't allow her coyness to distract his curiosity.

"When was this?" Brenda asked, nonchalantly.

"I remember you and Mama getting overly angry about Efe asking you about your children's father." Edward continued.

"Well that was a long time ago. Let's not talk about it now. It's a mood killer," Brenda concluded.

"Why do you always try to ward off this topic each time I bring it up?"

"Because I don't want to talk about it,!" she exclaimed in frustration.

"That's clear enough, but I don't know how far we can get with this relationship if you do not open yourself to me. I need to know more about you."

"Like what?" Brenda retorted, defensively. "That I was impregnated because of my foolishness? That my parents died because I had sent for them to see me? That I should have used my senses by not being at the wrong place at the wrong time? Or maybe, I should have just aborted that pregnancy!" Now she was crying.

Edward stood before her shocked. "How can you blame everything on yourself like this? How can you wish you had aborted those beautiful children of yours?"

"That's exactly why I don't want us to talk about this," she said, matter of factly. "The night is getting chilly, and I would like to go home now." She walked away without waiting for him.

"But we just got here," Edward called back, watching her waist twist as she moved in anger. She knew it would be a matter of time before she got to share her thoughts with him again if she walked away now, so she realized that if she did, indeed, value their relationship, that she needed to calm herself. They carried on, suspending the topic for then.

Three years later, Brenda married Edward. They moved out of Edna's home and into a bigger place with the twins. Edward's love for her children grew immeasurably. They began considering him as their father. After graduating from the University, Brenda decided to go into a boutique business in their town. In less than six months, her shop became the top ranking fashion store in town. She became very busy with her shop, so that she would return home late at night while Edward was left to fend for the children. The strong romance that brought them together was no longer there. On the other hand, Edward's business was flourishing as well, and he opened two more branches in the major city. He employed the best hands to assist in managing his marketing firm. As his business advanced, so his relationship with his wife withered. He began working from home to keep the children company. He also wished his wife was present most of the time to spend those moments together.

Too many nights he longed to make love to his wife, but she would ward him off because she was either busy or not in the mood.

As the days went by, Brenda also realized that she was no longer in love with her husband. The inseparable attachment they used to share was no longer there. Something was pulling them apart, and she had no idea what it was. As much as she tried to make things right, it just wasn't working. Something else was also bothering Edward more than his wife's attitude.

It got to the point where Edward decided to seek professional counseling. He waited for her to return from her shop one evening to discuss the idea. She walked in around eleven, and her children were already asleep. As usual, Edward was waiting in their bedroom with a remote in his hand as he watched the European football league. Without a word, she walked to him and pecked his cheek, but he didn't respond.

She decided to take a shower. Still motionless, Edward watched from the corner of his eye and deliberated on how to bring up the issue. He decided to wait for her to finish taking a shower before discussing. She walked out of the bathroom with trickle of water on her shoulder and a towel wrapped round her waist. She glanced at Edward as she rubbed lotion vigorously on her skin.

"Is anything the matter?" she broke the silence.

"Everything is the matter," Edward responded. "When you're ready, I'd like us to have a talk," he said, still staring at the TV. She went to the closet and brought out her night gown and slipped into it. She then crawled in bed and turned towards him.

"I'm ready," she said, with her hand on her chin, waiting for him to commence.

"I think we should see a therapist," he began. "I was speaking with a friend of mine who suggested a very nice lady out of town who can help us rebuild our marriage."

"Is there something wrong with this marriage? By the way, why were you discussing our personal problems with your friends?" she asked obdurately.

"Don't even go there," he warned. "We don't just have a problem, we need help. After all you always discuss our marriage with your friend abroad. This marriage is not working out perfectly anymore, can't you see?"

"If there's anyone who needs to see a therapist, it's you because you are the one always complaining and feeling insecure," she argued.

"I'm insecure? Ok let's talk about it then. How many times have you made dinner for the family in the past one year since you began your clothing business? How many times have you assumed your motherly role? Oh, let's not even go there. When was the last time we sat and talked like couples do? When last did we make love?" he demonstrated with his fingers.

"Is that all? If that's why we need to see a therapist then I see no issue at all. You are the one who has refused to see reason with me. I am extremely busy, and I thought you'd understand that. We are a couple and we are supposed to understand and support each other. We had sex last week. We have talked about this before, and that was why I asked Mama to find me a house help to do some of these things. In other parts of the world, men help their wives out with house duties and they still enjoy their marriage, but you are always nagging about one thing or the other."

"I'm sure the westerners at least endeavor to get pregnant after marriage."

"Edward, what was that you just said? So now it has gone into the issue of not being pregnant. You should have told me all along that this was what this conversation was all about, instead of mentioning a therapist!" Brenda retorted, turning her back to him and pulling the blanket vehemently over her shoulder.

"You always find a way to escape our discussion. We need to see someone if you still care about this marriage." He stared at her back, waiting for a response. He finally switched off the TV and lay down. He lay awake all night thinking about the discussion he just had with her and if his wish would ever come to pass. He glanced at Brenda who was deeply asleep beside him as if nothing was wrong. That infuriated him even more as he bit his lips and stared at the ceiling.

Brenda, on the other hand, was apprehensive. She didn't understand the reason for her childlessness. There was only one explanation; she was married to an infertile man. She thanked her god for giving her the twins. Whichever way, her family was complete. After a sleepless night of thinking, Edward fell asleep in the wee hours of the morning. Brenda woke up and sat up in bed and stared down at Edward who was sleeping. She felt this sudden hatred towards him. She wondered how she came to fall in love with him. She petulantly shook him. He turned to her and sat up confused.

"I was thinking all throughout the night and it came to me that what you need is not a therapist but a medical doctor," she said, vehemently.

"How do you mean?" Edward inquired as he tried to reason with his wife.

"It's obvious that you are the one with fertility problems and not me. I have two children to prove that, so if there's anyone who really needs an expert, it's you." Brenda snapped.

"But you know I've seen different doctors in the past six months and they all said that everything is fine with me," Edward protested.

"Then seek another opinion abroad," she said with finality.

Edward still did not understand the reason why she had woken him up this early to say what she did. He sat in bed and stared at her back as she left.

On the next Sunday morning, Edna arrived at her son's home unexpectedly and announced that she had come to take them to church. This was unlike her because no one had ever heard her mention a church, let alone attend one or to invite someone else. It was obvious that she needed a grandchild from her son by all means, and since she had been told by her colleagues at work about a miracle working pastor, she was anxious to see the signs and wonders manifest in her daughter-in-law.

Brenda disputed the idea at first but Edward pleaded that she attend the church service for the sake of their mother. Edna paced around the living room as the couple dressed up. When they were ready to leave, she was the first to approach the door as if there was something to be missed in the next minute if they weren't out of the house immediately.

"This man of God is a very busy one," she told them. "We must hurry before he finishes the first sermon. I was told that anointing flows during that period," she explained as she got into the driver seat of the car.

"Mum won't you let me drive?" Edward stared at his mother who had already started the car. She hurriedly got out of the driver seat and ran around to the passenger side and sat down. Brenda who was watching her the whole time burst into laughter. The family drove away from the compound.

As they all sat at the last row of the crowded church, they listened to the sermon blaring from the two heavy speakers mounted at the corner row of the church. The pastor roared and pranced around sweating heavily. The church chorused, "Hallelujah" and "Amen" at every word he spoke. A few women stood from their seats and began waving their arms in the air moaning and calling on the lord.

"They are filled with the Holy Spirit," a woman whispered to Edna when she saw her bewilderment at the organized scenario.

Brenda hadn't been to a church since her parents died. Her mum used to make them go to church even when her father was away for business. The church they attended was very different, and no one spoke until the preacher has concluded his sermon. For Brenda and Edward, the whole thing was intriguing.

After the first sermon, the pastor took off his jacket and handed it over to the usher who quickly brought him a glass of water. He gulped it down and began clapping in chorus with the tune the choirs were singing. He did a little dance and encouraged everyone to stand and dance as well. Everyone got up and began dancing. Kids rushed to the front of the church and bounced around. After the singing, the pastor began to meditate. The church was silent. The ushers roamed around the church hunting for those who had slept off during the meditation.

"Wake them up! This is the time the devil chooses its prey. We must not fall asleep. The children of God must not allow the devil to take control of them"

"Oh yes!" The church chorused, "we must not give in to the devil," and "the devil is a liar."

Brenda's eyes were gleaming in thrill as she listened to the church respond to the pastor simultaneously. She wondered why she hadn't been to church all her life. This was an interesting show for her.

"Ratata—butubu--ya ya!" the pastor rapped. A woman jumped from her seat and danced to the altar and began screaming. She rotated, twitched, and then fell to the ground. The ushers quickly picked her up.

"Our God is a living God."

"Amen!"

"I said our God is a living God!"

"Preach on pastor."

"And he will perform miracles today. He will loosen those in spiritual bondage, and he will shame the devil."

"Amen!" the church chorused.

"I see a woman. I see a woman whose heart has been shattered..."

"Oh, Lord," a lady whispered as she waved her large arms to the ceiling.

"This woman is in our midst today. She's been through thick and thin, but God has brought her here today." The pastor continued.

Edna who had heard so many interesting stories of deliverances in church, thought she was about to witness one herself. She stared from corner to corner, hoping that the poor woman the pastor was talking about would crawl out from her seat.

"This woman is here for something she already has. She is unhappy deep inside. Oh, Jesus, speak to me...speak in the language I'll understand...yes...yes..."

Brenda, like Edna, anxiously waited to see the woman the pastor was talking about. They all glanced around to see who would come forth.

"Brethren, please open your bible to the book of Mathew 6:14-15," the pastor ordered. Everyone began searching their bibles for the announced verse. "Can someone please read the word of God for us today?" the pastor asked as he glanced around the church. A middle-aged woman stood up with a worn-out, and unimaginably huge bible and began to read. One of the ushers dashed to her and placed the microphone inches away from her mouth. "If you forgive others their trespasses, your heavenly father will also forgive you. But if you do not forgive others their trespasses, neither will your father forgive your trespasses."

The pastor smiled at the crowd and wiped off the sweat on his forehead. "The Lord has spoken! Brothers and sisters in the Lord, this is the word of God, not mine!" As if the church did not understand what the verse meant, he repeated it this time slower, "...and if you do not forgive others their trespasses, your heavenly father won't forgive you."

The congregation nodded in response.

"Someone please read out Luke 17:3-4. Read aloud so the world may hear the word of God," he commanded again.

This time, a man stood up with a small pocket bible and began reading.

"Pay attention to yourselves. If your brother sins, rebuke him, and if he repents, forgive him. If he sins against you seven times in the day and turn to you seven times saying, 'I repent,' you must forgive him."

The pastor was mute for a few seconds and then resumed his preaching.

"Not to forgive is greater than sin. The bible condemns it. This woman with us has a heavy heart." He waited even more, his eye closed, his hands joined in front of his face touching his forehead and chin, his body swaying gently.
"

"If this woman does not wish to come forth for prayer, then I shall pray for her herear. Let the Lord heal her broken heart. Let the lord fill her heart with joy. In Jesus' name!"

"Amen!" The church clamored back.

Soon the prayer session was over and it was offering time. The band slowly began playing, and the hall was filled with loud music. Everyone danced in line towards the offering box and slipped in their offerings and tithes, then would go to shake the pastor's waiting hands. Edna and her family did the same.

Edna was so filled with joy that she grabbed the pastor's arm with both hands and shook them vigorously with a huge smile.

The pastor smiled and shook Brenda's hand as well. His face quickly changed while he was still holding her hand. He stared at her as if they've met before. "Please see me after service, madam," the pastor said to her, freeing her hand. Benda was concerned by the way the pastor stared at her. After the offering, the pastor rounded up with announcements and everyone left. In the rush,

Brenda forgot to see the pastor as requested. She mused over the fact that the pastor had decided to preach about forgiveness that particular Sunday.

But, she thought, it's easier said than done. It was a matter of circumstances and opinion.

On their way back from church, Edna kept smiling at Brenda and glancing at her son strangely. She seemed to be filled with the Holy Spirit. She began whistling the tune of one of the songs that had been sung in church and moved her head from side to side in sync with the tune.

Chapter 13

"Ma'am, the gentleman over there sent you this drink," the flight attendant whispered to Brenda who was absorbed in her thoughts.

"Who?" she inquired, peering into the quiet aisle of the airplane filled with passengers. She immediately saw a man waving enthusiastically four rows in front of her. The man got up and walked toward her. She wondered who he was and why he would send her a drink. It was an airplane, not a bar, and anyone was allowed to order drinks as much as they liked. If he thought it was some kind of romantic move, in her mind, he was mistaken.

As the face drew closer, she endeavored to remember where he had seen his face before. She gave a weak smile, staring inquisitively. She expected him to his intentions.

"Hello, my name is Andrew, and I've been watching you for hours now. You look worried, is anything the matter? May I sit please?" He introduced himself, pointing to the empty seat beside her. She still didn't say a word. She battled within herself to remember his face. There was an awkward silence as they both stared at each other.

"Oh...Ok. Nice to meet you Andrew...Thanks for the drink," she finally broke the silence.

"Are you traveling out of the country, or is this a connecting flight?"

"I'm a traveling," she replied impassively. This told the man that she wasn't in the mood for chit chats. She stared at the drink as the ice slowly melted in the glass.

"So where are you headed to?" he continued, but Brenda was inattentive.

"Ok. I'll leave you then. Sorry to disturb you," he said and got up to leave.

Brenda watched from the corner of her eye as he went back to his assigned seat. She got up and went to the rest room in the far end of the airplane. She gripped the seatbacks as she wobbled up the aisle as the plane shook slowly, passing over the Atlantic Ocean. It was almost chilly as passengers gripped their light comforters.

She noticed the red sign that declared the restroom occupied. She leaned on the hard plastic wall and waited. Soon a boy opened the door and came out smiling weakly at her. She went in immediately and bolted the door.

She moved the strands of her hair on her face towards her ear. She observed the corners of her eyes and chin and rubbed them gently. No wonder that man sent her a drink, she thought as she looked at her flushed face. Unsatisfied with what she saw, she pulled out a sheet of tissue and wiped the corners of her eyes as if it would eliminate the evidence of stress written all over her. She washed her hands and patted them dry with a clean tissue. She then walked back to her seat.

At first, she thought she was in the wrong seat when she saw Andrew seating on the empty seat beside her. She frowned and slumped onto her seat.

"Are you stalking me now?" she asked, scowling.

"No. I simply won't forgive myself if I ever leave a beautiful woman like you here alone soaking in your pain. I came back to keep you company. I saw tears in your eyes an hour ago. Maybe you didn't notice, but I was concerned. You may not be in the mood to listen to me right now, and I do not care to know what the problem is, but I am determined to put a smile on that beautiful face of yours till this plane touches the ground. Whatever you are going through, I've seen worse."

Brenda couldn't believe her ears and ogled him as he rambled. She tried not to stare at his soft lips that looked like they wanted to be kissed as he spoke.

He was average height with a fit body. The light grey sweater he was wearing made him look calm and business-like. His wrist watch and shoes announced some likelihood of wealth in him.

"I am sorry for my attitude earlier. I shouldn't be rude to someone with good intentions," she sighed at last. "I just have a lot in my mind, and I prefer to be alone. But it's a long flight anyway so I might just decide I've thought enough for the moment. My name is Brenda Akin.," she replied with a smile. She wondered why she hadn't taken time to look at him the first time he came to talk to her. He was going to be a good company, she thought. He reminded her very much of Edward.

"So may I ask what you are going after or what is chasing you?" he inquired playfully. Brenda pretended not to have heard his question but smiled to herself. "Okay, let me rephrase my question. Are you here for business, or pleasure?"

"None of them," Brenda retorted smiling.

"Then I guess you are running away from something?"

"You are very nosy. However, I'm just traveling to clear my head." The both of them laughed out loud. "Clear your head? I see. Why don't you start with the drink I offered you minutes ago?" he said handing her the glass of wine the hostess gave to her earlier.

"You have a good sense of humor you know," she said smiling and collected the drink from him and sipped from it.

"Then satisfy my curiosity. You seem to be thinking about something unpleasant," he asked again sipping from his own drink.

"Well let's just say I'm not in the mood to talk about it now."

After the church service her mother-in-law had dragged her and her husband to, she went into the kitchen to prepare lunch while Edna relaxed on the couch folding her *gele* – scarf, and the twins went to their rooms to play. Edward browsed on his laptop.

He heard a knock and went to the door. He hollered out loud when he saw his old high school friends who came to visit him.

Two men walked into the large living room and went to hug Edna who had wondered what the excitement was about. She recognized the two men to be Edward's high school friends. She got up and hugged them, looking them up and down.

They had just returned from Germany and decided to look him up. They sat down on the three-seater in the middle of the room. Edward hadn't seen his friends in 15 years. He stared at them in excitement. He called Brenda from the kitchen to introduce her to his friends. Brenda appeared with three wine glasses and two bottles of wine.

She observed them as they cracked jokes and reminisced about their high school days. They sipped their drinks and chatted. Edward was so happy to see his friends again. He listened with glee. He had run into Philip two days ago on his way to work and they hadn't had time to talk, so Edward invited him to his place. He hadn't expected to see Johnson as well.

"Nedu! *O'boy*, how did you manage to disappear when things were just getting interesting?" Philip, one of the men queried seriously.

"Mehn, *I won't forget our final year o.* You know before the final exams they replaced the principal. The new one became trouble.

"There was this issue about rape and pregnancy raining all over the school," the other man, Johnson, cut in.

Brenda's head whipped toward him at this pronouncement but said nothing.

"Who raped who?" Edward asked seriously as he poured the wine.

"Dude, you missed it all. You were lucky cus it was a very hot semester. There were dogs and policemen that looked like dogs sniffing around the school," Phillip responded.

"Oh my God, you still remember that?" Johnson interrupted bursting into laughter. "*Yes na.* Mehn, they stared at me like I was the culprit. Trust my *jango haircut* - - Shaggy hair cut *na.*" Philip demonstrated.

"So there was a rape?" Edward pressed.

"The story was that on that home weekend you left for the states, a girl was brutally raped. They said they found her in the school garden."

"Yes, a girl from the girl's school." Philip and Johnson narrated the story.

"So the parents hired the best in police investigation to sniff out the rapist. I heard they were very rich too."

"I won't forget the look on the principal's face when he came to announce it to the morning assembly."

Edward who had been enjoying the old school tales was suddenly filled with fear. He tried to hide his anxiety. "So did they ever find the rapist?" he asked.

"How could they when the girl couldn't even recognize him?" Philip cut in.

Brenda's ears burned as she listened to the story. She paled, but didn't move.

"I think they rested the case after many months. It was a coincidence that you left at the same time. If not, with that your bad boy record, you would have been an easy suspect."

"How do you mean?" Edward asked.

"I mean that you left the country when the heat was on. If I didn't know you, I'd say you were running away from something," Johnson concluded, jokingly, and the men burst into long laughter.

Brenda looked hard at Edward, feeling a wrenching in her stomach.

"But come to think of it," Johnson continued, "I still doubt that it was someone from our school. *I know say boys bad then but no be to rape girl na.*-I knew boys were bad then but not up to a rape," he said in pidgin English.

"John, you mentioned pregnancy earlier, was that another story too?" Edward asked.

Brenda continued to stare at her husband. Why was he so interested in the story?

"It's the same story. After the rape case was buried, I heard the girl was expelled when Lady Briggs found out she was pregnant."

"What? Why?" Edward asked angrily.

"Dude, a girl can't stay in school when pregnant, don't you know that?" Philip retorted sarcastically.

"I know that but,"

"But, what?" Johnson interrupted.

"Oh well, I guess it was the school policy, right, *but it's not fair na.* They should have allowed her to graduate knowing her condition." Edward replied calmly.

Brenda's stomach began to calm. Maybe he was just genuinely concerned, she thought.

"Lady Briggs..." Johnson echoed leisurely as he glanced at Philip.

"What about her?"

"Nothing. Just remembered her for Philip."

"Okay, guys, we won't go there today. Lady Briggs is history. I wonder where she is now?"

"Probably filing on young boys in the school."

"Wait a minute, so it was true?"

"What was true?"

"Oh, my God! So that rumor we heard then that you used to arrange Lady Briggs was true? You always acted like you didn't like her. That explains the constant trips to the girls' school then." Johnson teased.

The men let out deafening laughter.

"Nope, that's not true. She admired me and that's all," Philip defended.

"That's not what I saw. She either had a broken bulb or a ruined fan in her bedroom that needed some Philip touch. If it was a pro-bono, why wasn't I invited? Why didn't you ask me to accompany you on one of your handy-jobs?" Edward argued.

"You guys are just crazy. The woman liked me and that's all. OK. I give up."

"*Before nko, Wetin you wan argue* – Why would you argue it when we already have a proof?"

As they continued to share their past, Edward's mind kept going back to the story he just heard. If he was able to impregnate a girl back in school then that meant he was a father. He thought about how to inquire from his friends without seeming desperate.

"So guys, do you happen to know where the girl is from, her parents and all that?" Edward inquired. "Do you know where she could be right now?"

"Which girl?" they both barked simultaneously.

"Uhm...I meant the girl who was raped," he continued, blushing now.

"And you are asking us if we know where she is after 15 years?" Johnson snapped. "Why the sudden interest in her?"

"No there's nothing really. Just wondering what could have happened to her after the rape, just didn't seem right, you know,"

"Oh well. It happened and that's history now," Philip concluded.

"Do you guys remember when this bad boy here fought a boy in school because he wrote a girl he admired? Are you still that jealous?" Johnson teased Edward who smiled embarrassed.

The men burst out laughing again.

"I'll never forget that night. The principal couldn't wait to deal with him." Philip chipped in.

"*Una don kolo* – you guys are crazy," Edward replied. "At least I fought for what I wanted. What about the two of you, did you ever had the guts to ask anyone out?"

"*Eh-heh*, that reminds me, Johnson, are you still with Rita?" Philip queried.

"Which Rita?"

"Rita the one you stayed up all night writing love letters to." Philip teased.

"Yeah I remember that rude girl, but she was fine though." Edward testified.

"Well she traveled abroad after graduation and promised to write. I never heard from her again," Johnson explained.

"*Kai!* That girl really messed you up, bro. With the way you guys wrote each other, I thought you were gonna get married for sure," Edward teased and laughed. The men chatted a little while and left.

Chapter 14

Brenda had returned to the kitchen when listening to the whole conversation made her feel ill. She had momentarily forgotten about the rape, only to be reminded by these visitors from the moon. After the men left, she emerged from the kitchen with a glass of juice her hands shaking as she placed it on the table. Edward noticed her nervousness but delved back into his own thoughts of what his friends told him. After all these years, his sins had come to haunt him.

Brenda was woken up by the gentle voice of the captain who announced their current location and weather status. She had been listening to Andrew for a long time and dozed off leaning on him. He, too, was asleep with his head resting on the window frame. She quickly sat up, rubbed her eyes and peeped through the window. It was dark, and all she could see were the red blinking lights on the wings. She had been in the air for three hours.

She suddenly felt a need to stretch her legs, but another look at the handsome man sitting beside her weakened her legs. She wanted to be cuddled. She just didn't know why she was suddenly attracted to this stranger on the plane. She gently snuggled closer to him and rested her head on his warm shoulder, shutting her eyes. She felt his arm gently wrap round her waist. She wanted to enjoy that comfort while it lasted.

Edward couldn't sleep. He kept thinking about his friends' revelation. He hadn't felt such guilt in his life before. He thought he had escaped the crime he committed years ago. He began to question himself. His heart beat faster. He got up and went to the mini bar in his living room. He poured scotch into a glass and gulped it down immediately. He moaned at the warmth of the drink traveling down his throat.

He rubbed away the tears in his eyes as he gazed into empty space. He did not notice Brenda standing at the door leading to the living room. She had been watching him. She walked up to him and stroked his head. Edward could no longer hide his tears and pain, and wanted the comfort of his wife. It was the first time she had touched him in a long time. He quickly wrapped his arms around her.

"Do you want to talk about it?" she asked, solicitously. He said nothing as he held her tight like a child.

"I am ashamed of myself. I am not worthy to be called a man. I did something despicable, and not even God may be able to forgive me," he sobbed. "Perhaps, I am being punished for my actions with childlessness."

He knelt before her. She was speechless as she listened. "I raped a girl 15 years ago while in high school and fled. There is never a day that I don't remember her screams. It was an awful thing. I did not know what got into me but I am very sorry. I am sorry that I didn't tell anyone, I am sorry that I never told you, my wife. I just suppressed the memory for so long."

Brenda pulled the collar of his shirt and buried her face in his chest crying. Edward stroked her back, thinking that she was grieving for him.

She pulled back, now cold. "I overheard your friends discussing it. I wasn't sure from the conversation that you were the one responsible. How could you?" she queried, holding her emotions in. She had waited for 15 years for that moment but her reaction wasn't as hostile as she had planned them to be, if she ever found him.

"I need your strength right now," Edward said, sobbing again. "I need you to help me find her. I have to seek her forgiveness. I have to."

"What will you tell her if you find her, that you are sorry to have put her through all that misery? She also has your children you know. Will you demand to take them away from her?" she asked coldly.

"I don't know what to say to her now," he said, still oblivious to Brenda's pain. "But when I see her the words will come. I just have to apologize. I need to clear my conscience. I need to find her."

It started to dawn on Edward that his wife wasn't showing him the sympathy he expects.

"Such a coincidence," she began, mockingly. "I was raped 15 years ago by a boy I didn't know. I lost my parents few months after. I was kicked out of school. My aunt felt I was a prostitute and would be a waste of money to send me to school. I was pushed out of her house on a rainy night in my nine month of pregnancy. And don't get me started about my inheritance which I also lost to my aunt and her son. A woman came to my aide. She took care of me and my twins. Years later I was married to her son. Today he kneels before me to plead for forgiveness. What type of a calamity is this? What joke is God playing on us?" she cried, angrily.

Edward's blood shot eyes widened as she lamented. Now the picture was becoming clearer to him after all these years. He quickly pulled away from her as if she was a ghost. His heart began to pound in his chest as if it would escape from his mouth.

"You demand for forgiveness now because your friends told you she was pregnant. Why didn't you look for her to apologize when you returned from abroad if forgiveness was so very important to you?" Brenda queried.

He swallowed his tongue in search of what to say. He should have thought about that himself, instead of waiting for his wife to remind him. To him, he felt this showed he was inconsiderate and didn't deserve to be forgiven.

"I am very sorry, my love. I am only human and I agree I did you wrong. You never told me the circumstances of your rape. Mama never told me; no one told me!" He slumped down to his knees again and crawled to her bosom crying.

"Please forgive me. God, please forgive me. Brenda, forgive me,"

Brenda couldn't control her tears and shifted her gaze away from him. "Please look at me. I am begging you." he cried, trying to refocus her attention on him by gently guiding her jaw. He then noticed the twins standing at a corner. They watched the short drama between their parents.

"Mum, what is going on here?" Richard asked as he drew nearer.

Brenda stared at Edward who held on tightly to her bosom.

"You and your sister should go back to your rooms. I will tell you later," he ordered. Edward quickly got up with his face covered with tears to go and hug them.

"Forgive me," he whispered to the children, who were completely confused by the conversation.

"Don't drag them into this!" Brenda barked. "Leave them alone. Don't rub this shame on them."

Brenda walked over to him while he was still kneeling down. A surge of anger crossed her face as she stared at her children. They quickly went to their rooms. She turned to Edward who was sitting on the floor like a child. She spat on him as tears rolled down her cheeks. She stepped over him on the floor and went into her room.

The next morning, Edna was invited to their home by her son Edward. He wanted her to help plead with Brenda to forgive him. He felt she was the only one his wife would listen to.

Edna finished listening to his son narrate what he did years back, and she jumped up and pounced on him.

"*Chim ooo!* –Oh my God! This is an abomination. What have I done to deserve this sacrilege? Who raised you like this? Where did this come from? Do you know what this poor girl went through? Do you know it almost cost her future, her life, and you --- *you* caused the death of her parents too. How dare you sit there to tell me this story? You better make peace with your God," she screamed and went over to Brenda who had been watching the whole thing.

"My daughter," she clucked to Brenda in an attempt to soothe her. "It was not by luck that I ran into you that night with your pregnancy, it was by fate. God wanted it to end this way. I will not support evil. Your husband here has wronged you. *Biko,* – please, my daughter, forgive and forget. My knees are on the ground for you. I am sorry."

"No," Brenda screamed in near hysterics. "No! It was not God's will that my parents died in a ghastly car accident and I was blamed for it. It was not God's will that I marry the man who brutally raped me. I will never forgive him and I won't stay in this marriage either. It will only remind me of my experience." She suddenly was quiet, then said, evenly. "There is murder in my heart after all these years of harboring this injustice" Brenda replied, "and I am holding myself calm to keep me from committing what is in my heart."

"Please, my daughter. Our elders say that we don't solve problems when angry. I understand you are very angry and I support you. Did you remember the story I told you years back about my own life? Please do not allow the past to ruin your future. I have seen this happen, and it never turns out well, dear heart. Please forgive. You have every right in the world to be furious, but my dear, for the sake of your children, look at them, and please don't leave now. You need each other more than ever. Please, I beg of you, my daughter."

Brenda looked pityingly upon her mother-in-law, the woman who had been a mother to her and grandmother to her children. "I need some time alone to think," she said. "I will be leaving for the United States in few days. I plan to leave the twins behind, and I shall be back for them when everything is settled. I need time to think, *mama*. I will always love you like my own mother, but this marriage will not work. I regret marrying your son. I've always hoped that one day the rapist would come forth, but I didn't expect him to come from my own family. I think you can understand my shock. We'll continue to be a family as always. I'm sorry, Mama."

Brenda got up and went into the next room. Edward tried to go after her but his mother restrained him. "Let her be for now. You've caused enough damage already."

The pilot had just begun his announcements as the lights came on. Everyone stretched and yawned in tiredness. The plane was set to land in ten minutes. From the window, one could see the bright lights of the city and the airport runway. Soon the plane's wheels slammed on the ground and sped for a couple of seconds till it slowed down. It began rolling slowly to its gate. Brenda who was enjoying the company of this stranger now wished the plane hadn't landed. She wanted to see him again. She hadn't felt such connection to anyone in a long time.

Although she was still hurt, she still felt there was a part of her that was willing to take another chance. "I guess we've arrived," Andrew whispered in her ear seductively, her head still leaning on his shoulder. "I want to see you again. Can I call you?"

Without hesitation, Brenda fished out a pen and a piece of paper from her purse and scribbled a phone number in it.

"I will be connecting from here to Delaware for a business, but I will definitely give you a call before I return to UK."

"My cell number," she smiled and handed him the paper. He smiled, collecting the paper from her and stuffed it into his trouser pocket. I will call you," he replied and got up still staring deep into her eyes. He walked to his assigned seat and began collecting his things from the seat pocket.

As soon the plane came to a halt, impatient passengers scrambled for their luggage and soon the small aisleway was filled with people waiting to exit the plane as soon as the door was flung open. Brenda waited another ten minutes before she could leave the plane safely. She turned around for the last time to see if Andrew was still in the plane, but he was already gone. She walked into the terminal and headed to the baggage claim hall. She waited for her luggage to appear, and dragged it away, steeling herself to face the customs process.

Toni spotted Brenda a long way off. When Brenda called Toni telling her about the fight she had with Edward, she invited her to stay with her till she sorted things out.

Brenda walked outside to meet Toni who had been waving in her direction. They ran and hugged each other. Toni led her to the car, and they drove away.

Toni and Brenda arrived in front of a big mansion with a fountain in the middle of the grounds which were nicely surrounded with well-trimmed flowers. The lawn was no exception as the sprinkler added to its beauty that early in the morning. Brenda was intimidated by the striking beauty of her friend's house. It was more beautiful than the one she grew up in that people always spoke about. She didn't want to seem timorous to her friend so she removed her attention grounds and cheerfully followed her friend's lead. She walked through the huge living room which was heavily furnished to the taste of a celebrity. The flat screen TV was placed on a mahogany stand with a sleek DVD player underneath.

Honey colored Italian leather secluded the entrance to the living room and the corridor. There was a hand-crafted vase of Chinese design. The green and red flowers in the vase complimented the cream colored curtain which floated on a puff of air from the heating vent behind the couch located near the window.

A stuffed tiger placed grandly in the center of the room on a Persian rug caught Brenda's eye, appearing so real. Brenda couldn't hide her amazement as she stared at everything in the room.

"You live here alone?" she found herself asking Toni.

"Yes I do now, but come let me show you to your room so you can freshen up," Toni replied smiling at her friend's dumbfounded reaction. Brenda wanted to think about Toni's response about saying she lives there alone, but ignored it for now till she was settled.

Brenda followed her through another corridor that led to the stairs. They marched to the first floor and went around, circling the living room, stopping before the last door in the hall. Toni opened the door and beckoned for Brenda to walk in first. She watched as Brenda's mouth flew wide open as she entered the huge bedroom with the bed in the far end of the room beside the window. There was a black fluffy rug beside the high bed four poster bed.

A small flat screen TV was placed in the opposite corner of the room.

"This is grand," Brenda beamed.

"I hoped it would suit you," Toni beamed back.

"Suit me? I adore it!" Brenda replied throwing herself on the soft queen-size bed that sunk deep beneath her weight and bounced back quickly sending thrills of excitement to her body.

"How do people live like this and still worry?" she asked rhetorically.

Toni shrugged her shoulders. She then went over and turned on the air conditioning. "Now you can enjoy better," she teased. "I'll be downstairs in the kitchen. Why don't you freshen up and meet me there?" she ordered Brenda, who was still lost in the thrill. She didn't even see Toni leave the room.

After a fabulous breakfast which had been prepared by Toni's cooking staff, the two of them returned to Brenda's room.

"Has he called?"

"Has who called?" Brenda wanted to know.

"Your husband."

"He's not my husband. That rapist is not my husband!"

"I know how you feel but has he called you?"

"You have no idea how I feel," she retorted. "He has not called, and I don't expect him to."

"Don't you think you are taking this thing too far?"

"is that what you think for a man who raped me and ran away? If my father was alive, he would have shot him like a dog."

"I just think you shouldn't have left without your kids," Toni advised. "Have you even called them to see how they're doing – how they're taking this?"

Brenda turned to look at herself in the mirror as she arranged her hair. "No, I haven't. I'll call them tomorrow."

"Look, Toni" Brenda said, glancing at her friend and then looking back in the mirror. "I believe I did the right thing. Those kids have paralyzed me for years. I can't even think of myself as simply a young woman because I feel like I've always been a mother. I'm not even 30 yet, and I have two children half my age. Now we know who their father is, and they have their grandmother as well," she spilled all at once. "I just feel like I need a goddamned break for once in my life."

"I just want you to be happy, Brenda," Toni said with concern as she turned to leave the room. "Just know I'm here for you."

Chapter 15

Edward was in his office when Philip entered wearing a long face. He hadn't been himself since Brenda left. It was so obvious that even his friends could smell his sorrows from afar. He avoided their weekend nights out because he was ashamed of telling them what he did that made his wife leave. Even if he didn't want to discuss it, they would make him share his problems. Philip decided to visit his friend to find out what was going on.

"Why didn't you tell me?"

"Tell you what?"

"I got a call from your mother this morning. She told me everything. Where is your wife now, has she contacted you yet?"

"Why did my mum tell you? Women, can't they ever keep their mouth shut?"

"That's beside the point, Nedu, you kept your mouth shut for too long, and this is where it has landed you." Philip called his nick-name, retorting sarcastically.

'No. She wouldn't talk to me. I don't know what to do. I brought her so much pain, and now she has to face me for the rest of her life. So I understand why she left. It's my cross to bear."

"Tell me again what you were thinking to have committed such a crime. You were lucky her father didn't find you when he fumed like an enraged bull. But why did you let her go, why? You shouldn't have allowed her to step out of your house. You should have begged until you fainted if that was what it would take to make her forgive you."

"She has forgiven me. She said she needed some time to think. "

"She had to go all the way to America to think? I guess she told you that so you wouldn't have to restrain her."

"My brother, what would I have done? I didn't know what else to do. I know she will be back. I know she still loves me. Brenda and I have come a long way, so I believe things will be fine between us."

"In your dreams," Philip said, restless and bored of his friend's weak protestations.

"If she doesn't forgive me then that will be my cross to bear, after all I caused her pain for fifteen years."

"You need to start thinking ahead. Yes, you wronged her, and I'm sure I would do the same if I were in her shoes, but how long are you willing to allow her stay out there vulnerable and angry at you?" Philip asked.

"Are you suggesting I go to America and drag her back?"

"No you don't have to. But you will have to court her all over again. Find out why she fell in love with you at first. She may be stubborn now but keep trying. Send her a gift, a very useful one that shows you miss her and want her back." Edward listened to his friend blame him further but advised him as well. He rubbed his head and face gently. "Get up. Let's go have lunch. We'll think of something while we eat." Philip pressured. Edward stood up, grabbed his car keys from the table and left with his friend.

Over lunch, they concluded that he should send her a laptop so they could communicate easily. Philip thought perhaps if Brenda saw her children from the screen that it would change her mind to return to them. It sounded like a well thought out plan to Edward, so he ordered the laptop and had it delivered anonymously to her.

After months of living with Toni, Brenda felt it was time to move out to her own home. She had watched her friend argue on the phone with numerous women both home and abroad whom she thought was sleeping with her husband. Toni began to realize that the man she had married was in demand more than she thought. He would spend days outside the country with numerous women. He would throw parties every now and then without inviting his wife, instead inviting other girls and his team members. Toni would find out from the papers.

Toni had decided to file for a divorce shortly before Brenda arrived, but didn't want to tell her because of her friend's own delicate situation. Knowing what this would do to his career, Toni's husband began sending threatening letters and phone calls to her. She made several police reports and vowed to continue with the divorce.

Brenda had woken up one morning to hear Toni talking with a man she later introduced her as Alex. He was her best friend. He visited every now and then to find out how Toni was dealing with the divorce. As Brenda walked down the stairs to the kitchen, she overheard their conversation.

"I sent out these documents for verification to my friends out of state. You will be stunned to hear what they discovered."

"Alex, right now I'm not interested in whatever they found out. I just want to get this divorce done and over with," Toni said, irritably. "I'm guessing it's another affair with another woman abroad?"

"Far from it, hun'. You don't wanna walk away empty handed do you?" Alex explained further. "Just take a look at these papers and tell me what you see."

Toni collected the papers and scanned through them. "I don't get it," she blurted with a frown.

"Look closer dear, concentrate on the digits at the bottom," Alex encouraged.

"Are you saying he has over ten point one million dollars hidden in Australia?"

"That's not all. He used a different name for that account. The second account is in Nigeria," Alex continued.

"Yes I'm familiar with the one back home," Toni defended. "You mean this one with 5 million naira?"

Alex pointed to a line beneath the paper. "Yeah, but it's more than what you are showing me here. That's because the account was opened after you got married."

Alex drew closer and whispered to her. Toni's eyes widened. "That bastard! He lied. He presented only the five million from his American account to the lawyers."

"Well now you see for yourself," Alex confirmed. Toni saw Brenda's image in the mirror opposite her.

"Come Brenda, come and take a look at what this man is doing to me."

Brenda drew closer as if she didn't hear the entire conversation. She collected the papers and gently sat down, covering her legs with her night gown pullover. Without a word, she stared at Alex and turned her gaze to Toni.

"Are you sure this is correct?"

"Yes, Alex brought it."

"I know but you're sure there's not an error somewhere? I know your husband is rich but this is just preposterous."

"My ex-husband," Toni chipped in.

"Yes, your ex-husband," Brenda corrected herself.

"Well, now you know how rich he is," Toni snapped angrily.

Alex who had been watching the ladies argue about the information suddenly stood up and told Toni he had to run. Toni walked him to the door and hugged him. He in turn pecked her on the cheek. She watched him get into his car and zoom off the vast compound.

"Oh I will fight him. I will fight that bastard to the last penny," Toni fumed as she returned to the couch.

"You have to let your lawyers handle this you know." Brenda advised.

"He has already convinced the lawyers that he had just five million dollars, and they are ready for a deal. Don't you see that he would easily deny those papers even before I present them?"

"That's why I said you have to let your lawyers deal with it. That way they would run more investigations and then pin him with this."

"To think he wanted to play with my intelligence. I think I better call him now."

"No you shouldn't. If you do, he will quickly move the money elsewhere and you will lose at the end."

Toni thought for a second. "There's truth in what you just said. I better contact my lawyer then."

"Exactly. Do that and go from there. Men are just too sneaky. "

As the fight between Toni and her ex-husband wore on, it became worse with threats of burglary and threatening notes. She wondered how her friend got involved at first with such a dangerous man. Brenda also became close to Alex who visited every evening and brought videos to watch. She knew he was gay but didn't want to ask him about it. She just enjoyed his company and laughed at the way he paraded himself when talking.

Brenda didn't want to be dragged into the whole charade, so she decided it was best to move out and still keep her friendship with Toni and Alex. She found a job at a local post office, just a few minutes away from where Toni lived and also found an apartment close by a month later. The postal job had nothing to do with what she studied in the University, but she didn't mind it as long as it fed her and kept her comfortable till she was ready to return home.

One evening she was watching TV when her phone rang. She glanced at the screen and couldn't identify the international number that displayed on it. She reluctantly pressed the answer button and listened for the caller to speak. She didn't recognize the voice at first, but smiled widely when she realized it was Andrew, the man she had met on the airplane on her way to America.

She had waited for his call for the past six months since she had arrived in the U.S, but decided he must have either forgotten about her or lost her number. She couldn't hide her excitement as she spoke loudly on the phone.

"Why did it take you so long to call me?"

"Well, I would have called earlier if I knew you were expecting my call," he teased. Brenda felt shy and smiled. She always admired his sense of humor.

"I'm sorry it took this long," he continued, "but believe me, there was no day I didn't think of you. I was so occupied with work demands that I totally lost touch with reality," he explained.

"Since you finally remembered me, you must have been fired," Brenda retorted sarcastically. They burst into deep laughter.

"No, I am actually in Hong Kong overseeing a new project my company is handling." "It's good to hear from you again, Andrew."

"It's good to hear you, Brenda," he said quietly. "Do you have Skype capability," Andrew asked. "I really want to see your lovely face."

"Sure. Let me get my laptop." Brenda quickly pulled out the new laptop from under her bed where she had hidden it. She turned it on and waited for the screen to come online.

"Are you online now?" Andrew inquired.

"Yes, I have a Skype account. I use it to talk with my children. What is your username?"

"I'm sending you a request now."

She accepted his request, trembling in her excitement to see him once again. Soon she received an invitation to view a webcam. She quickly accepted it and waited for the face to appear. There was his handsome light skinned face with a light, well trimmed mustache on his chin.

"Turn on your webcam so I can see you," he urged. Brenda with mouth wide open quickly turned on the webcam for him to see. "Well," he responded coyly. "Aren't you looking as beautiful as the first day I saw you on that plane with tears in your eyes?" he teased.

Soon her home phone rang again and this time it was Edna calling. She quickly grabbed the phone and yelled, "Hello?"

'How are you, my daughter?"

"I'm fine, Mama," she responded calmly. "How are you and the twins?"

"They are fine and worried. They want to know when you'll return home."

"Mama, I will return soon. Send my love to them." She flared up, biting her fingers as she spoke.

"Why have you abandoned your family for so long? Haven you no heart of forgiveness? Do you think your parents would be happy to hear that you have decided to abandon the one thing that should bring you joy?"

"Mama, please don't bring my parents into this. I have to sort out my life first. I want to clear my head from your son's abomination."

"But he's still your husband!"

111

"That's why I need more time to think. I will call you tomorrow; take care of yourself and the twins. Send my love to them."

She hung up. She had no plans to return to her husband or children. She had finally gotten an escape and felt she had to take advantage of it before she got any older. She wanted to see the world and enjoy her life before going back to her family. Brenda returned to the waiting screen with Andrew's handsome face on it.

They began talking and viewing each other on webcam. She forgot all about her activities for the day. She didn't want to leave this man for any reason. The more time they spent chatting the more she liked him.

Brenda would leave work every day and run home to chat online with Andrew, to tell stories and even model for him. Her friends noticed her sudden diversion and queried her a couple of times to tell them who had been occupying her mind lately.

The Internet romance that started on an airplane grew into a deep love affair. Soon he invited her to London for a visit. She was thrilled about meeting this man who had stolen her heart away. She always felt that if things work out for her and Andrew, she would immediately file for a divorce from Edward for good. Days later, she received a flight e-ticket which had been paid for by her lover. She hurriedly excused herself from work for two weeks and prepared for her trip. Toni accompanied her as she shopped endlessly in every store she knew. Everyone could sense her excitement but she wasn't prepared to disclose her love affair to her friends.

On a chilly Friday evening, Toni accompanied Brenda to the airport. Everyone turned to look at Brenda parading in her dark blue jeans and yellow top with a silver lined hill slippers. She was somewhat anxious about her trip as she had agreed to spend two weeks with almost a complete stranger.

She glanced at her wrist watch a couple of times. The airport wasn't really crowded as it would be on a Christmas morning or Valentine eve. She was happy not to wait in line for too long. She felt the cool air from the air conditioner on her face and hair. She turned around to hug her friend who stared at her worriedly.

"It's not too late to cancel this trip you know," Toni suggested.

"Only in your dreams, Toni. I've always believed that what will be, will be. If it turns out bad then I will return and if it turns out good..."

"Then you will file for a divorce from Edward?" Toni interrupted sarcastically. "I still wish you'd return to him. You've punished him enough. That's worse than going to jail. What if this man—this Andrew--is not what he claims to be, what will you do?"

"Then I will return like I said. I have to go now before I miss my flight," she concluded glancing at her wrist watch.

"You still have one hour before your flight, but I understand if you do not want to talk about it. Enjoy your trip. Call me if you need anything," Toni replied, walking away.

Soon Brenda was standing behind twenty people at the checkpoint. The line went as fast as it could even though the security guards often had to recheck people and even take them aside for some questioning concerning the items in their luggage. She knew that once she crossed that line, she would have to face anything that would come her way. After an hour, they began boarding the plane. She found her seat beside the window. She sat and looked out, seeing the darkness outside with red lights on the runway. She felt a sudden excitement in her belly. She smiled to herself and other passengers who were still boarding the plane. After another thirty minutes, the pilot at last announced their departure.

Chapter16

The plane landed at the Heathrow airport in London six
hours later. As usual, passengers trooped into the
terminal and headed towards the empty baggage claim.
Brenda read the directions on the lighted boards in the
airport. She took the escalator which led her to the
baggage claim hall. She lifted the light-weight luggage off
the roller and dragged it gently down the hall.
Soon she was out in the crowded terminal with arrivers
swimming in and hugging their families. She stood in the
middle of the hall and glanced around the room in search
of Andrew, but he was nowhere in sight. She walked
further towards the exit and looked around but didn't see
him. Disappointed and nervous that he might not show
up, she walked to the money exchange boot and handed
the man in inside a twenty dollar bill. The man announced
how much it was worth in British pounds. She wasn't
prepared to bargain at that point. All she needed was a
coin exchange to use the phone.
She quickly grabbed the exchanged bills and coins off the
wooden desk and walked to the phone boot dragging her
luggage along. She brought out her diary and searched for
Andrew's cell number and began dialing it on the public
phone. She waited for him to pick up the phone but it
went to voicemail. Her heart began to race. She decided to
try it again the second time and this time he picked up the
phone.
"Where are you?" she barked, frowning.
"I'm sorry I was caught up in traffic. I should be there in
fifteen minutes. I'm coming," he said.
"All right," she responded, relaxing a bit. "I'll be in
the...the..." she looked around and gave him the name of a

nearby airport bar where she would wait. She could see the airport entrance from there.

Fifteen minutes rolled to twenty. Finally, forty-minutes later, she saw a tall guy running into the airport and looking around. She recognized his face and quickly stood up. She called out his name and ran to hug him, leaving her luggage on the floor. He kissed her long and hard. She broke from him and stood to take another look at his handsome face. He smiled at her and lifted her luggage from the floor, and they both walked towards a waiting taxicab.

She was surprised that he came to pick her up with a taxi, but she decided not to mention it. He grabbed her hands and kissed them gently. She was confused but pleased at the way he treated her. He was everything she thought she wanted.

The taxi pulled over in front of a brick bungalow outside of town. The street smelled dirty from wet cigarette butts littering the sidewalks. The part of London which she often saw on TV looked nothing like where she was about to spend two weeks of her life. But she felt it was too early to judge him in any way. *Worst case scenario, she consoled herself, he probably lives a decent life despite the neighborhood.*

He paid the cab driver, jumping from the cab and walking towards one of the doors facing the street. He began searching for a key from a jumble of keys in his hand. Brenda gently got out of the cab and stood behind him, waiting for the door to be unlocked. He threw the door wide open to a scantly furnished small living room and ushered her in. She gazed around the vomit color painted wall and the tiny kitchen that looked like a hall way with a rough wooden shelf on the wall that looked precarious. There was only one pot and a frying pan in the kitchen. It looked like he had cooked before coming to the airport. He distracted her with a light touch to the shoulder, leading her towards the bedroom. She climbed the long, narrow stairs gently which led into a small bedroom with double twin mattress on the floor. There were only two pillows on the bed with fading cream colored sheets which were pilled from too many washings.

A small table in the corner of the room held two wristwatches and a faded silver necklace. She had disappointment written all over her face. This was not the type of house an international consultant would live at. This was nothing of the expectations Andrew's demeanor had sparked. She barely knew anything about this man aside from his feelings for her.

"You live here alone?" she asked.

"Yes. I just moved in here two months ago. I used to stay with my friends but the place got too uncomfortable for me I moved out. I'm still putting things in place. Forgive my mess; I'm still fixing it up," he replied, hugging her from behind. She knew she loved him too much not to tolerate the unbearable environment she was in.

Before she could ask another question, he had started kissing and undressing her. She felt a tingle in her spine and couldn't resist the tender touch of the man she flew thousands of miles to see. She allowed him to take control of her body as she hugged him tightly. He laid her on the mattress and she felt the roughness from the pilling on her back and elbow. She adjusted herself to avoid being distracted from his touch. The bulge in his trouser aroused her more and she couldn't wait for him to take her. He undressed himself, revealing a well toned torso and muscular arms. They indulged in long kissing and foreplay before he began banging her ferociously. She enjoyed every bit of his touch that she held him tightly, wrapping her legs around his waist.

After the first round of sex, he quickly went to the bathroom to clean himself. He pulled on his briefs and marched down the stairs to the kitchen. He grabbed a cigarette he had hidden in a pot, slipping it into his mouth and lighting it. He blew the thick smoke in the air and went to the fridge and brought out a bottle of beer and began to sip it.

Brenda who was done with her shower smelled the cigarette and rushed downstairs. She watched him puff and blow the cigarette smoke in the air with slow resolution.

"You never told me you smoke"

"Yeah I do sometimes *yah*. I thought I told you on the phone when you asked me."

"No you didn't. I don't think I would have forgotten something that important."

"Does it bother you?"

"Yes, I really don't like smokers."

"Ok, I'm sorry, I won't smoke again," he capitulated.

Brenda again made a shocking and disappointing discovery about the man she thought she loved. He had presented himself properly during their chats, so that one would think he was the perfect and classy gentleman. She went back to the room, stomping up the stairs. She was very tired and wanted to rest before she could face him fully.

She was already beginning to regret her trip but her return ticket wasn't until thirteen days from now. She could either pay a two-hundred dollar fine that the airline required for a ticket change or wait it out. Perhaps, she thought, she wasn't really paying attention to the good things about him. She lay down on the bed and dozed off few minutes later.

She had slept for a couple of hours when she felt a nudge behind her. She turned around to see Andrew smiling seductively at her. He had been touching her body in her sleep and she seemed to be enjoying it but was still too tired to respond to his urges. She smiled weakly and tried to pull herself away from his strong leg on her thigh, but he grabbed her and began kissing her again. She couldn't resist this time but knew that he was about to snuff out the little energy left in her.

He took her again and his vigorous hammering felt stronger than the first time. When he was done, he rolled to his back and dozed off. Brenda tried to fall back to sleep but the noisy rants from the neighboring apartment wouldn't let her. She got up and slammed the window shut to prevent the noise but was forced to reopen it because of the intense heat that occupied the little room. After a while, Andrew got up and went over to where her box was lying and unzipped the first pocket layer and brought out her laptop. He searched for the charger on the side pocket and brought it out. He woke her up from her *little death* and demanded she give him the pass code or unlock it. Not really trusting him, she felt it would be wise to unlock it herself than giving it to him. She gently sat up and collected the laptop from him. She squinted from the bright light on the screen. She searched for the keys and punched them in. When the welcome screen came on, she passed it over to him and watched what he was doing. He browsed the site, waiting for her to go back to sleep. Too tired to protest, Brenda obliged him by quickly returning to sleep.

The next day, she woke up very early and rushed down to the kitchen to make him some breakfast since it was a Saturday. She opened the old refrigerator and glanced around in search of eggs. When she didn't find any, she called him to come and show her where to get some. He came down to meet her in the kitchen and went to confirm himself that there were no eggs in the fridge.

"Um, can you just go and buy some?"

"Uh, sure," she said, uncertainly. He told her how to find the nearest market, and she waited for him to hand her money.

"Oh," he said, nonchalantly. "Can you buy them with your money because I don't have any cash with me now. I'll pay you back as soon as I get back from work."

Brenda stood there mouth open in search of what to say. "Okay," finally escaped her mouth. She went up the stairs and took out her purse and squeezed out the rest of the pounds she had exchanged at the airport. She went back downstairs to meet him waiting at the door.

She walked briskly to the store and bought the items she needed that morning. She went back to the kitchen and began to prepare breakfast. Her heart was heavy with anger and disappointment. She felt great dismay at his behavior. She just hadn't expected this from him. She tried to hide her feelings.

She felt obliged to stay with him despite her state of mind. She remembered Toni's warnings about her trip. She hoped that another day would be better than the present one. After their breakfast of fried plantains, eggs, and hot chocolate, she decided to check her email. She ran up the stairs and grabbed the laptop which Andrew had left on the floor last night.

She brought it downstairs and sat beside him. She waited for the screen to come up so she can unlock it. She typed the web address of her mail server, and realized that Andrew had forgotten to sign out of his account. She knew he wasn't watching her, so she decided to go through his email. Her eyes caught some sent messages which piqued her curiosity. She would wait until he left for work so she could read it properly. This was her only opportunity of really finding out more about him more than he had ever told her.

She opened a new web page and began browsing the net.
When he noticed she was carried away with her browsing,
he pushed closed the lid of the laptop and began smiling
at her. He demanded that they go and shower together. He
brought up the idea of a bubble bath. He gently took her
laptop from her and placed it on the table and lifted her
from the couch. She couldn't help but giggle as he
marched up the stairs with her in his arms.
When they got to the bathroom, he gently put her down
and began undressing her. She let him. He poured some
bath liquid in the tub and filled it with warm water. He
lifted her into the tub and climbed in behind her. She
leaned on his chest as they both sat in the filled tub. He
caressed her neck while she ran her fingers on his legs.
"You know, women always feel like they wash themselves
properly, but they don't." He began.
"How do you mean?"
"I mean, do you always wash your vagina, I mean really
inside your vagina?" he blurted.
"I don't understand," she said with a quizzical look. "I
believe some women wash their body parts properly but
no one can sponge the inside of a vagina. It's like asking if
someone can ever wash the inside of their ears. Medically
it's not even advisable and it could be..."
"Says who?" he interrupted. "Well there's a Q-tip for that.
My friend's girl friend used to squeeze weed in there to
bring to boyfriend when he was locked up in Surrey. So
don't tell me nothing can get in there except a penis." he
grimaced
"Well I don't know what your friend's girlfriend had in
mind when she transported weed in her vagina, but all I'm
saying to you is that it's not healthy to sponge inside a
vagina. If one gets a scratch there, they could easily get an
infection. It's a sensitive part of a woman's body..." she
debated.

He was less concerned about her medical reasons than for not agreeing to his suggestions. He continued to scrub her back as he persuaded. He kept nodding his head sardonically. He then turned to her and spread her legs and tried to squeeze in a wash cloth in an attempt to show her what he meant by washing a vagina. She quickly clasped her thighs and got up with a frown.

"Are you out of your mind?" she barked at him. He laughed scornfully and watched her leave the tub with water dripping from her body. It dawned on her that the man she had been talking to and had obviously fallen in love with was nothing close to the man she was visitng. She was more ashamed of herself than before. She picked up a towel and walked into the bedroom.

He got out of the tub and went to meet her in the room. He held her and began apologizing. She cheered up, but in her mind, she knew this visit was a very grave mistake. The small town where he brought her to was empty and had nothing much for a tourist attraction. He lived on the outskirts of London, and everything in the little town was boring. She wanted to see more. She had heard so much about the city of London with its shopping malls and street boutiques. She wanted to sit in the double-decked bus; she wanted to see Trafalgar square, feed the pigeons, and see the ever-stoic Buckingham palace guards outside the palace and tower.

All these things she had envisioned seeing with her loving boyfriend, but she realized this was only a fantasy and would never come true. It was four hours away to get to the city where everyone who visited England would wish to be. She begged him to take her to London so she could witness the city herself, but he gave excuses about how long it would take to get there, and how expensive the train ticket would be for a last minute trip. He promised to take her to a better place in town.

She sat in the lonely park and watched kids play, while Andrew texted on his phone. This was not the fun touring in London he promised her. She watched a girl and the boy slide down the pole. It reminded her of her own children back in Nigeria. She hadn't mentioned anything about her marital life to her lover. She felt when the need arose, she would spill everything. She needed to get to know him first. Her life detail was a heavy secret to disclose to a stranger. She didn't want to scare him away with her dirty secret either.

She thought about Edward who had tried contacting her after she left for the United States. It had been nine months since she left, and she had vigorously opposed any attempt her mind made to recall the memorable experiences she had with Edward. A part of her still loved him, but she felt her lack of forgiveness was not enough to punish the man who put her through the greatest misery of her life.

She wanted to experience life; she wanted to fill in the missing dots in her life. She wanted to feel alive, fall in and out of love, to experience the life of a young woman before child bearing.

What had Edward been up to she wondered. Could he be having an affair with someone else? Would he make her children call another woman mother while she was still alive? She asked herself.

She was instantaneously recalled to her present situation by the wandering hands of Andrew squeezing her shoulder. He drawled closer and nibbled her ear. As if he knew what she was thinking, he drew her closer and said, "I'm sorry I may not be what you expected, but you know, I'm just as baffled as you are. I mean, in the webcam, you looked really younger and your curves were so sexy, but when you visited me and I saw your stomach, it made you look as though you had had children. The pictures you sent me were totally different from you right now. I'm not disappointed, just not what I expected. Look at your cheeks," he teased, pulling her cheeks playfully, "they are chubby. Chubby cheeks...hahaha!"

It was the height of it for Brenda who stood up and marched back to the ugly brick bungalow. She had never been so humiliated in her entire life. She bit her lips and cried as she marched in anger.

Reaching the bungalow, she packed her bags and called the airline and rescheduled her ticket. Andrew didn't bother to follow her, and she called a cab to take her to the airport. The taxi driver arrived ten minutes later and she quickly jumped into the cab, threw her hand bag in front and continued to cry. She waited a few hours at the airport before she finally boarded a flight back to Boston. He never emailed or called her to apologize, nor did she expect any contact from him. She wondered about the sweet, ever loving Andrew who would sit on the phone for hours talking to her, and how he seemed to suddenly change to this obnoxious, sarcastic and narcissistic man. She couldn't bear her heartbreak anymore nor the pressure from her mother-in-law who called her everyday to remind her of the treatment she was giving to her son. Some days she would call to say, "He talks about you even in his sleep. He vowed not to see any woman until you return. He is devastated. He is sorry, my daughter, o...*gbaghalu*. Can't you see what you are doing to my son?" and Brenda would listen to her rants and then end the conversation with, "send my love to my children, Mama".

Deep inside her, she knew she had punished Edward well enough, but the pride in her rebuffed the thoughts. She still had this anger buried deep inside her that none of Edward's pleas could suppress.

Chapter 17

Weeks rolled into months as she kept busy with her post office front desk job. One afternoon she had just returned from her lunch break and found a post card from Andrew. He had written to say he was sorry and looking forward to better days with her. This short note made her realize how much she was tormenting herself, and most especially her family. She realized that the adventurous life of a spinster she had dreamed of wasn't beautiful after all. She missed her children more and wished she never found out about Edward's identity as her rapist.

Edward sat in the bar with his two friends, he kept quiet as they discussed. The music was blaring and it only irritated Edward the more. He wanted to prove to his friends that he was ready to date again, so he agreed to meet them that night for a drink. However, he still couldn't shake his feelings for Brenda whom he hadn't heard from in a long time.

His friends noticed his absent mindedness, and Philip tapped him on the back.

"Are you with us?" Philip asked. Edward nodded. "You've been quiet ever since you got here. Did Mariam do anything wrong?"

"Who's Mariam?"

"The blind date girl. You told me you guys hit it off instantly," Johnson remarked.

"Oh, yeah we did. It's not her. I'm just tired, that's all."

"You didn't even remember her name. Look at you, look at yourself in the mirror, you've grown old already. She's out there having the time of her life while you are here wasting your life away," Philip barked. "You need to forget her man. It's been a year already and she doesn't love you."

"She loves me. She's just angry" Edward defended.

"Angry for a year now? Don't you think that's enough sign for you to see that she just wants to be rid of you?" Philip argued.

"She is still my wife. Yes we have our issues but we will sort it out, with time…"

"So what about Mariam? What about this beautiful and down to earth girl that has been taking care of you all this while?" Johnson queried.

"Mariam was your idea, not mine. I have no feelings for her. I am still married and can't have extra-marital affair."

Philip sighed. "If you're still so in love with Brenda, why don't you go to America to visit her? Pay her a surprise visit. Who knows she might see that you are truly sorry?" Philip proposed.

"I agree with Philip, you may need to do that," Johnson chimed.

"And what if she refuses?" Edward inquired, giving a thought to his friends' idea.

"What other proof will you need to know that she doesn't want you anymore?" Philip retorted.

"Just come back home and be with Mariam. She will make you happy," Johnson said, shrugging at Edward's question.

Edward gently grabbed his car key which was lying on the table and hugged his friends. He then left the bar and drove home. He thought about his friends' suggestion and felt they were right. He just had to keep trying. Who knew, she might change her mind.

It was the night before Christmas and many offices had already closed early. The city was gaily decorated and the lively tinsel belied Brenda's feelings. The colored tree lights twinkled on the small trees in the city square. The small shops were beautifully lighted in response to the season.

The wind blew erratically as a light snow began. It was the probable weather for Christmas in the Northeast. Men and women held hands as they walked in out of the malls; children tagged along their mother, clad in puffy down coats fit for the weather. Cab drivers in a hurry to deliver their passengers and also rush home as well, honked endlessly at the many drivers trying to weave their way off the heavy traffic on the route 28 expressway.

Brenda wasn't much into Christmas decorations. She knew that children loved Christmas trees and their twinkling lights, and most importantly, the joyous Christmas spirit it brought to the home, but the thoughts of her own children shifted her interest in whatever Christmas entailed. She had shopped in the nearby supermarket that evening for something to cook for herself the following day, since her friends had traveled to be with their own families.

Even as much as she wanted to be with her family, she couldn't place herself in the family picture; her children were the most important thing to her, but the fear of returning to Nigeria to be with them and then having to stare into those puppy eyes of Edward's--ever pleading for her forgiveness for the slightest of slights. She didn't want to look into them nor hear him plead before her. She had always tried to analyze her stubbornness but always comforted herself by thinking that he deserved every treatment she dished out to him.

As she squeezed the fresh oranges into a small glass cup, she realized how lonely she was that night. She had planned to call Edna and her children to wish them a happy Christmas, but the thought of listening to them query her when she would return made her heart sink.

She quickly gulped down the liquid and dumped the empty orange rinds in the bin underneath her kitchen sink.

She returned to her living room and turned on the TV. She searched the channels for something interesting to watch, when she saw flashes of a car headlamp through her window. She gently peeped out into the dark parking lot and saw a man dressed in a white shirt with young people beside him. Not expecting any visitors at that time of the night, she pulled her curtains together and returned her gaze at the TV.

There was a knock at her door. It was a little late for carolers, she thought, but couldn't imagine why anyone else would be on the street on Christmas Eve. She stared at the door, straining to imagine that the knock was on her neighbor's door. But the knock came again, this time louder.

She stood up slowly, dropping the remote in her hand and walked inquisitively towards the door. She peered through the hole in the door but it was too dark to see a face. At last, she opened the door and beheld Edward and her twins standing at the door shivering. She quickly took her children by the hand and walked into the living room and pulled out a blanket she brought out earlier to keep herself warm. She wrapped the blanket around their shoulders and hugged and kissed them.

They looked so different from the last time she saw them. She couldn't believe she had stayed away from them for that long. Without a word, she lifted her face to look at Edward who stood by the corner of the door still holding his briefcase. He quickly shifted his eyes from her and went to bring in the rest of their luggage from outside. Brenda stared at the two large bags he dragged in and immediately regained her awareness.

"What are you doing here?" she asked, cautiously.

"The kids and I wanted to surprise you by coming to spend Christmas with you. It's okay if you do not want me to stay. I have the cab driver's phone number. He will drop me off at the hotel."

"Do you know how dangerous it is traveling with these children by air and arriving by this time of the night?" she queried in other attempt to find a way to blame him.

"Honey, it's only 9:00. I called your number several times since I wasn't too sure of the address. I think I copied your address wrongly, so we've been driving round town looking for the right building, not until the cab driver suggested..."

"That made it even riskier! What type of a stupid surprise were you planning dragging my children into? This is completely unacceptable," she interrupted.

"In other words, you propose we leave your house?"

"No. You leave! If this was a coy to get me back as your wife then you are out of luck."

"Divorce me then. Divorce me if you do not want me. What type of a woman are you? Why are you so hard hearted? These children are the only reason why I'm standing here today. I owe them everything. I dare not complain about your arrogance because I've accepted all blame. What else do you want from me? What can I do to make you see that I am very sorry? Tell me," Edward charged as he grabbed her arms.

Tears rolled down her cheeks. "I came here to escape you and my pain. I love my children but the thought of their father sickens my stomach. I didn't bargain for it."

"Look at you. You stand there and say all these hurtful words before your children? You treat me this way before them? Do you think your parents would be rejoicing in their graves when you speak like this?"

"Don't you dare bring my parents into this. You caused their death. You put me through this misery. You caused everything."

"Fine! I did. I accept every blame you throw my way, but I'm sorry my love. I would rewrite everything if I could. I just want to make things right. I just want your forgiveness. I want us back like we used to be. Please Brenda, I beg of you. I sat for eleven hours on that plane not just because I wanted to surprise you, but to seek your forgiveness." He knelt before her and clutched her legs.

"Get out. Leave this moment," she bellowed.

Edward stared hard at her and lowered his face. He gently stood up and leveled one of the suit cases on the ground. He unzipped it and revealed some home-made food items neatly wrapped and the photos they had taken the first time he took her out on a date. 'Here...Mama sent these. She thought you might need some food stuffs, and the twins brought this hoping you will remember what we used to be like before all these madness," he said handing her the food items and the photo frame. She collected the items and dropped them on the table beside and continued to stare at him. "I will be lodging in the hotel close to the airport, and I shall change my ticket so I can go back tomorrow as well. I am sorry for showing my face here, and ruining your holiday," he said quietly.

"They will resume school in two weeks, so please send them back on time. I promise you will never see me where you do not want me, again. Have a nice Christmas," he said and went to hug his children.

"Daddy will see you very soon. Richard, take care of your mum and your sister. Make sure you have lots of fun and take lots of pictures to show me when you return. I love you," he whispered, then got up and grabbed his suitcase and left.

Brenda watched him walk down the cold and quiet street. He turned to look back but continued walking. She watched him disappear into the dark night. She turned to her children who were glaring at her.

"Mummy, why didn't you let him stay for the night?" Rachelle queried.

"Your father did me wrong and you must accept that. It cost my parents their lives as well. You are not to speak about this issue ever again. Go into the room and change into something warm. I'll go and make you some tea."

"Mum, we know everything. He told us everything. We've forgiven him and you should do the same. You've punished him enough and we are not happy about this." Richard retorted.

"Shut up, you brat! What do you know about forgiveness? Who taught you to speak like this?"

"Mum, we are fifteen years old," Rachelle said. "We are not children. I do not see anything wrong with what my brother said. Either you call our father back, or we will go with him tomorrow. Even if you are our mother, I think you are losing it."

At that moment, it dawned on Brenda that those little children she used to cuddle and rock to sleep every night were no longer children. They'd grown into teenagers with a mind of their own. A bold and disrespectful mind as well, she thought.

"You kids don't understand..."

"Make us understand, Mum! Make us understand how you've emotionally tormented our father. He waited for you day and night, and even refused to hang out with his friends because he didn't want them to convince him to date someone else. He didn't want to come on this trip with us. It was our idea that he come to make peace with you, but it seems you do not want him after all. What about us, can't you forgive him for our sake? I am so disappointed in you, Mum," Rachelle cried.

"You have to go and call him back, or we will leave and you will never see us again," Richard snapped. Brenda stood there staring at her children as they yelled at her. She hadn't seen them in a year and they had obviously learned a lot without her. They had also grown so independent and far from her expectations. They seemed to hate her without a second thought.

"If only you both knew what I passed through while pregnant with you..." she cut short what she was going to say, and sighed and walked to the kitchen.

"Mum, you have to bring him back. It's not safe out there. How could you have asked him to leave this night, when it's snowing heavily and he has nowhere else to go to," Richard yelled, beside himself.

As Edward walked past the bright lighted city, he decided to hail a cab instead of calling the former driver that dropped him off earlier. "No one deserved to be bothered on Christmas," he thought. Each cab he hailed was either out of duty or packed with people headed to a party. He thought about calling a friend who lived hours away from Massachusetts, but the thought of having to explain why his wife threw him out of her house at that time of the night was shameful. Most importantly, to narrate his ordeal to his mother who had advised him against the trip, would be humiliating. All he wanted at that moment was to get to the hotel, take a shower and sleep.

His journey hadn't been successful but he could do with a warm meal as well. To think that Brenda didn't even offer him a cup of tea hurt him the most. He was lost in his thoughts when a cab strolled up beside him. The cab driver rolled down the passenger window, "do you need a ride to town or do you plan to walk your life away? I've been calling out to you for some minutes now"

"Yes! Yes! Sorry, the Courtyard Marriot near the airport."

"Oh, Buddy. There's a lot of traffic between here and there, stopped on the freeway trying to get downtown. Let me see," he placed his finger on his lips for seconds, to think. "I think I know another way to get there. I might have to cut through Milton and to 93 north highway. It may cost you slightly more, but it's Christmas so..," the man replied and looked at Edward to catch his expression.

"All right. I don't mind," he interrupted and yanked the door of the cab open, threw his bag in, and sat down in the warmth of the cab.

"Going to a party?" the driver asked cheerfully.

"No."

"You must be working tonight, then?"

"No, I'm not." Even though Edward wanted to chat with him, his mind was still occupied with Brenda's reaction towards him that evening. He regretted his trip. All of a sudden, he felt this wavering hatred for her for the first time. He frowned at the rash judgments that crossed his mind.

"Are you married?" he asked the driver. "No but I'm engaged."

"Don't even try it," Edward said, bitterly. "Half of the world is in pain because of women. Even in the bible-- it began with Adam and Eve," Edward advised the driver who frowned at him. He tried to lighten the mood.

"True! Women are tough but where would a man be without one?"

"Happier and maybe even peaceful."

"Wow! You must be really unhappy to have such opinion about women?"

"Yes I am."

The cab driver turned his attention to Edward's lament. "I believe no matter how angry a woman is," the cabbie continued, 'if you buy her a gift and apologize, things will be alright. It's as easy as that. You might get a slap on the first day of apology but later on, you will learn your lessons. That is, depending on what you did to her," the driver chipped in.

"Of course, my fiancée in Mumbai always accused me of flirting with other girls," the cabbie prattled on. "The other day she called to tell me she had a dream about me and another woman in matching attire walking round the furnace seven times. So I decided to prove her wrong by buying her an engagement ring. I plan to propose to her when I travel to Mumbai next week. Maybe that way she would stop having nightmares about me and other women. Trust me, she would start singing a different tune. You see how difficult yet easily appeased women are?" the cab driver explained jovially, chuckling as he drove and gestured with one hand.

Edward paid little attention to what he was saying but needed the distraction. He just wanted to stop thinking about Brenda for a moment and this cab driver was helping him do just that.

"You see, that's the problem. At least your fiancée dreams; my wife is angry. She's been angry for years but didn't know whom to place it on, not until I came along. I wish I was slapped and forgiven later. Maybe I wouldn't be sitting in this cab with you chatting away like this on Christmas Eve. I should be with my family, you know? Guess what? I am going to sleep in a hotel room tonight; I am going to take a shower, have a drink and then sit and cry away my pain. You know why I want to cry? Because I'm tired of everything. I am tired of begging for her forgiveness. Like a slave in chains, I've been restrained from my own feelings. I do not even have a right to be angry; I dare not complain because I made her that way. But guess what, driver? I don't care about anything anymore. If I die today, God will know that I did my best in seeking her forgiveness. I am not the worst person on earth," he complained as his lips quivered in anger and sorrow. Tears gathered around his eyes, and the cab driver listened to him as he narrated.

The road was slippery from a light snow that had fallen hours ago. The temperature had dropped to freezing. The driver was concerned about him and continuously glanced at his rear view mirror to look at his face.

"But whatever that is causing you this much pain should be removed from your life entirely. That is what I read in a book. A book I bought days ago. It says that we should not let things that don't matter to determine the things that do."

"Brenda matters. She's my wife, the mother of my children..."

"But you are unhappy. You are crying, and she's not here to see that. When a man cries then it must be really a big issue. You need to get hold of yourself. You need to calm down. I know a place to take you to cheer you up, if you'd like to go. There are lots of beautiful girls there. I'm sure you will like at least one of them. Trust me, they are really beautiful. I know one from Bengali..."

The taxi sped along the scanty highway, its wheels skimming the surface of the wet, slippery road. The cabbie bent to get a box of tissue that was lying on the floor of the taxi, but didn't notice the trailer that was speeding towards him. He diverted to the opposite lane, during which he lifted his face to wheel back to his lane, but he crashed into the trailer on the other side of the road. By the time the emergency response team could arrive, Edward was already dead. He was rushed to the hospital

Burning Wind

where they tried to revive him so many times but he gave up the ghost. One thing was obvious; he died with tears still in his eyes.

Chapter 18

       Two policemen showed up at Brenda's door on Christmas Day to ask her to accompany them to the hospital. She was confused at first about their mission until they mentioned Edward's name. The twins ran outside to hear to what the officers had to say. Frantically, Brenda dashed into the apartment, grabbed her purse and ran out. Even though she didn't care much about what Edward had to say, a part of her still loved him. The twins asked to accompany her, but she assured them everything was fine. She rode in the same car with the policemen and arrived at the hospital.

       She walked briskly behind them and still confused as to what Edward would be doing in the hospital. If it was another way of gaining her sympathy, he would only be wasting his time, she thought. She walked through the vast hallway and waited for the elevator which arrived seconds later. She entered, accompanied by the officers. She didn't realize how worried she was until she stared at the mirror in the elevator. She noticed the tears gathering in her eyes. Her hands were shaking and her mouth was dry. Her heart beat faster as if it would jump through her mouth.

       The elevator traveled down to the basement. She thought it odd that they would have patients in the hospital basement, but thought perhaps he was in the emergency ward. She followed the officers towards the quiet and creepy hallway that led into a large cold room. A heavily bearded man in his fifties appeared with a white coat and a large reading glasses on his face appeared. The officers whispered something to him. He stared at Brenda with pity and asked, "Madam, are you sure you want to do this?"

"Do what?" she asked.

"Are you sure you want to identify him?"

Still confused, she covered her mouth with her palm, not knowing what to expect. She began to be afraid. The man walked over and pulled aside a drape. He left it open and stepped aside for Brenda to see.

"I'm sorry madam." he whispered as Brenda broke into a loud cry.

She saw Edward who was lying shirtless and dry, with no atom of life in him. She stared for an instant, but couldn't bear it for too long.

She turned to run out and ran squarely into the bearded man.

"Is this your husband, ma'am?"

"Ye-es. No. Yes," she said, crumpling and sobbing.

"Thank you," was all the man said as he pulled the drape in front of Edward's body.

A nurse stood waiting for her and directed her to another floor where she would receive instructions for the disposition of the body.

"How...how did he die?" Brenda asked between sobs. The woman told her matter-of-factly of the cab accident.

Her feet were too heavy to carry her as she began thinking of what to tell her children. How was she to disclose that the man who had brought them to spend the holiday with her, died suddenly in a car crash?

Too numb to tend to details at the moment, Brenda returned home, announcing to her children that they would be returning to Nigeria in a few days. They asked her what had happened, but she refused to disclose the terrible story to them. She was afraid they may do something outrageous, judging from the argument they had the night before the incident, but how could she deny the visit by the police. She knew it was only a matter of time before they sniffed out the truth. She wasn't prepared to deal with another loss.

Rachelle who was the closest to Edward kept asking her all throughout the night what had happened, but Brenda assured her that everything would be fine. She wished everything would be fine like she always promised her children.

Brenda wasn't as frantic as she expected, but she was filled with guilt. Whatever it was that strengthened her heart after the death of her husband was extraordinary. Even though she blamed herself for his death, she still felt it could have been prevented if he didn't come with the children. She maintained her stand that Edward's own stubbornness led to his untimely demise.

Toni came to help her make arrangements to transport Edward's corpse back to his home town. The paperwork was completed in a timely manner by the airline authorities, to transport Edward's body to Nigeria, but Brenda worried about what would happen when she got there. Toni pleaded to accompany her for the funeral, but she refused. She wanted to face the consequences alone because she knew about Toni's ordeal with her own husband and knew things wouldn't be favorable if she traveled with her.

Toni dragged Brenda out of the room where her twins were seated, to her bedroom and shut the door. She pointed to her bed and asked her to sit. Brenda sat and wondered what was in her friend's mind this time. She wasn't prepared for a discussion about anything. Toni stared at her for sometime then placed a hand on Brenda's knee and tapped it twice.

"Don't pretend everything is alright. I know you and how you feel about the incident but if you wear this face to

Nigeria, your late husband's family will tear you apart. You need to take this incident seriously. It is a calamity."

Brenda made to interrupt her, but Toni hushed her with a wave of her hand. "I'm not done yet. I know you want to defend yourself about this one but no one knows you better than I do. I have been married longer than you have, and, although I've dealt with a great deal of betrayal from my husband, I didn't let it take control of my life. You pushed this one too far. I will be remiss if I allow you to believe that his death was just. He didn't deserve it.

"If I don't tell you now that you've lost everything then you might probably think I'm joking. I am sorry for your loss my friend but please be careful when you get there. Your in-laws will not be kissing and hugging you when they see you."

Brenda froze as she listened to her friend. "You blame me as well? You think it's my fault he's dead? Even you, Toni?"

"I am not blaming you, I'm only telling you the facts, Brenda. You are my friend, my best friend at that, but you pushed this one too far."

"I can't believe this is coming from you." Brenda argued. She needed her friend to support her.

"Brenda, look at me," she grabbed Brenda by the jaw and searched her eyes. "You must admit to yourself once and for all that you pushed it too far. I am being very honest with you as a friend. I know what he did, and I don't support his actions, but now he's gone. You can't blame the dead."

Toni was determined to get everything off her chest. "A dead man is as pure as the day he was born. The least you can do is to prove to your children that you didn't intend your actions to have this result. After this funeral, you may lose everything, but just know that I am here when you need me."

Brenda breathed a sigh, then rose to her feet and went back to the living room. It seemed like no one was interested to know why she behaved that way. It was pointless speaking to her friend who seemed to have joined the blame-band.

As they sat on the plane, she became paranoid. In her mind, everyone seemed to be staring at her. She also felt like she was hearing whispers about her from the passengers behind her. She wondered if they knew what she had done, and if they also knew the truth of the story to judge her. She needed them to understand her own side of the story. She stared at the twins who were quietly seated beside her; Richard had his IPod earpiece in his ears while Rachelle dipped her eyes into a teen romance novel she bought at the duty-free book store at the airport. She didn't expect Rachelle to speak to her, since she barely conversed even during a normal situation. One could only imagine what is going on in her mind right now.

Brenda knew there was a lot to worry about if her children were already isolating themselves from her. It was very important to her that they believe her. Her worries settled as the plane floated thousands of feet above the ground. She dosed off a couple of times and would awake from a nightmare in which she had seen Edward's face in the morgue. She then turned to see Richard's glaring eyes on her. This worried her the most.

"Do you need anything?" she muttered.

"Do I have to need anything to stare at a heartless woman? I worry for you, Mum," he retorted.

"Don't speak to your mother like that again, boy," Brenda barked.

"You think we don't know what happened? You've finally killed my father. Pray Grandmum doesn't have your head as well."

This infuriated Brenda the more but also worried her. Her children were turning against her and she didn't like it. She pinched him on his back. This made Richard moan out loud in his seat. People turned to stare.

"Pinching me won't change the fact that you caused the death of our father. Why don't you explain that to Grandma," Richard blurted as he rubbed his back gently, absorbing the stinging pain from the pinch.

Brenda turned and caught Rachelle's eyes watching the two of them, and then she returned to her novel. Brenda began wiping the tears from her eyes.

"Your father died in a car accident. I wasn't there when it happened, neither did I invite him to America. You both make it seem like I caused his death," she explained.

Richard ignored his mother and plugged his earplugs back into his ears. He didn't want to hear a word of what his mother had to say. To him, she was looking for a way to defend herself.

The flight seemed longer for Brenda and her children than they had ever experienced in their lives. If it was in her control, Brenda would have chosen not to land, and not now that everything seemed hot. Her heart began racing as her children hurriedly squeezed past everyone on the plane and disembarked without her.

The warm temperature at the airport worsened her anxiety as sweat trickled down her forehead. She gathered her belongings and walked out peering through the crowd to catch a glimpse of Edna and Martin, probably waiting with a gun, she thought. She consoled herself that it would not be possible because it was an airport and no one was allowed to enter with any form of weapon. However, the trip to their home was still far enough for anything to happen. She feared Martin could harm her on their way home. She knew the incident was unforgivable.

Soon she saw her twins embrace Edna whose eyes had swollen from crying.

Edna lifted her face to see Brenda, who had stopped in the middle of the terminal to stare at her in terror. Edna lifted the edge of her wrapper and wiped the tears streaming down her eyes. Brenda was touched at the woman's state. Edna bent and whispered to the children who nodded in response and walked away with Martin. He had been standing there glaring at Brenda and her melodrama.

As she drew closer to Edna, her lips quivered and she quickly slumped to her knees crying. She caught the attention of onlookers who circled around them in morbid curiosity.

"Mama..." she began but her lips seemed too heavy to speak.

"We have a car waiting to transport him to the mortuary. Hand me the papers so I can get going." Edna spoke wearily as she looked down on Brenda who was on her knees, ignoring her plea.

Brenda scuffled through her purse and brought out two sheets of papers stapled together. Her hands were shaking as she placed them on Edna's waiting palms. Edna turned around and walked toward the information desk at the airport, and a cheerful woman dressed in a white shirt and black skirt collected the papers from her. She picked up the phone, dialed a number and spoke in it. Few minutes later, a man in a blue vest and black pants appeared and led Edna towards the narrow hallway. Brenda stood up and walked briskly after them.

The car drove straight to the mortuary as arranged while Edna, Martin and the twins rode in another car. Brenda was too terrified to ride with them in the same car, so she hailed a cab from the busy airport.

When Edna and her children arrived home, she instructed the gateman not to allow Brenda in. Brenda's cab pulled up to the tall black gate minutes later, but Etim, the gateman, appeared and delivered the message as instructed.

She jumped from the cab, shouting for her children and banging on the gate, but no one came for her. She turned around and instructed the cab driver to take her to a hotel.

The next day was a cold Saturday afternoon as Edna's family, friends and colleagues gathered to console her on her loss. The twins snuggled close to their grandmother who cried as she listened to her friends. Then she stood upright, wiping the tears from her eyes.

Onwu bia egbu. Onwu ibiara be m? – Death, have you come to pay me a visit again, have you?

Ariri erigbuo la nu mu o – My heart is heavy with thoughts.

Edward *nwa m o* – My son,

Ebere emegbuorala mu umu ya o – I worry for his children. I worry for what their fate would become.

Umu nna, nwa m anwuo la nu – My people, my son is dead.

Edward *nwa m, kedu otu isi hapu m*? – Edward, how can you leave me like this? How can you abandon your mother like this?

Kedu ka Iga esi hapuru m umuaka a? – How can you abandon your children like this?

Chi m ino kwa na ahu ihe a? – My God are you witnessing all these?

Onwu gburu mama m – Death took my mother years ago,

Gbuo umunne m, gbuo nna m – Took my siblings and father,

Onwu chukwara m bia ebe umu m no – And now death followed me to my children.

Chi m, onwere ihe mmere biko gwanu m. – God, if I ever wronged you in any way please let me know now.

She sang mournfully as she rocked her body and slapped her laps over and over. She turned to her guests in tears as she lamented. One of the women came to her side and patted her on the shoulder. Another woman helped wipe the tears from her eyes. The door opened gently as Brenda walked into the large living room where some people were seated and some standing as they listened and talked quietly. All gazes shifted to her. There were murmurings as she drew nearer.

Edna jumped up to her feet and pounced on her. She grabbed the collar of the black cotton top she was wearing, choking her. Brenda struggled to free herself from the old woman's grip.

"Have you come to laugh at us? Have you come to rub this shame on my face? How dare you come into my house, did I not instruct Etim not to let this woman into my house?" she accused as she shook Brenda vigorously. "Where is Etim?" Edna raged.

Brenda was quiet and then began to cry. She felt pity for the woman she had caused so much pain. She had never seen her in so angry. Edna was Brenda's only family.

Martin stood up and held his mother, pleading with her to let Brenda go.

"She killed my son, your brother, and you want me to leave her alone? *Umu nna, o kwa nwanyi ojo gburu nwa m. Okwa Nwanyi ojoo a gbulu Nedu.*--- My people, my son died in the hands of his evil wife." Edna sobbed mournfully.

The murmurings increased as Brenda knelt down before her. She crawled on her knees to a man she knew to be Edward's father and pleaded with her eyes.

"He pleaded for your forgiveness; he walked on his knees; he cried like a child, day and night, yet you still wanted his blood. Now you've finally killed him, please leave us alone!" Edna raved, throwing her arms up in the air.

"Mama, no matter what I did, I deserve to bury my husband, at least to pay him my last respect," Brenda spoke as she sobbed.

"So now he's your husband? Didn't you abandon him to go and date other men while you were in the states? You think we didn't know?"

"What happened was between your son and me. I'm still married to him so please don't push me away," she argued.

"Get out of here before I have you thrown out," Martin barked. "You are so ungrateful. You bite the hand that fed you. He is dead; leave us to our sorrow."

"What more do you want from us, you ungrateful wretch," Edna cursed.

"I must leave with my children then. Richard...Rachelle..." she called out.

146

"Which children?" Edna asked, coolly, "The ones I raised from the moment they were born? Please leave this place."

The dramatic scenario took a new turn when Richard got up and began pushing Brenda out of the house. Rachelle buried her teary face in the belly of her grandmother, refusing to look at Brenda. The noise increased in the room as Brenda turned and walked away. She didn't expect such reaction from her children.

After Edward's funeral, Brenda had known there was only one person to help her out of this mess she got herself into, and that was herself. She realized she must forgive herself first before seeking other's forgiveness.

Brenda went back to the US without seeing her children again. She wrote them a couple of times with no response. She called so many times but Edna told her not to contact them ever until they were of an age where they could decide on their own whether they wished to see her or not.

Brenda knew that forgiveness was far from her reach but hoped that someday she would make peace with them. She knew she would have to live her life without forgiveness, but most importantly, without Edward's forgiveness.

The End.

Burning Wind

www.ingramcontent.com/pod-product-compliance
Lightning Source LLC
Chambersburg PA
CBHW030615130626
46552CB00002B/580